THE
STARS
BENEATH
OUR
FEET

David Barclay Moore

ALFRED A. KNOPF
NEW YORK

THIS IS A BORZOI BOOK PUBLISHED BY ALFRED A. KNOPF

This is a work of fiction. Names, characters, places, and incidents either
are the product of the author's imagination or are used fictitiously.
Any resemblance to actual persons, living or dead, events,
or locales is entirely coincidental.

Text copyright © 2017 by David Barclay Moore
Jacket art copyright © 2017 by R. Kikuo Johnson

All rights reserved. Published in the United States by Alfred A. Knopf,
an imprint of Random House Children's Books, a division of
Penguin Random House LLC, New York.

Knopf, Borzoi Books, and the colophon are registered trademarks of
Penguin Random House LLC.

Visit us on the Web! randomhousekids.com

Educators and librarians, for a variety of teaching tools,
visit us at RHTeachersLibrarians.com

Library of Congress Cataloging-in-Publication Data
is available upon request.

ISBN 978-1-5247-0124-6 (trade) — ISBN 978-1-5247-0125-3 (lib. bdg.) —
ISBN 978-1-5247-0126-0 (ebook)

The text of this book is set in 11-point Miller Text.
Book design by Maria T. Middleton

Printed in the United States of America
September 2017
10 9 8 7 6 5 4 3 2 1

First Edition

Random House Children's Books supports the First Amendment
and celebrates the right to read.

For
Brian Patrick Moore,
a star if ever there was one.
I miss you.

WE HAVE NOT MET ON EARTH AGAIN,
AND SCARCELY SHALL; THERE DOTH REMAIN
A TIME, A PLACE WHERE WE SHALL MEET,
AND HAVE THE STARS BENEATH OUR FEET.

—Richard Chenevix Trench, "The Story of Justin Martyr"

1

What I couldn't get out of my skull was the thought of their rough, grimy hands all over my clean sneaks. What I couldn't get out of my heart was this joy-grabbing stone I felt there. Partly because of these two thugs trailing me now, but more because I knew Jermaine wouldn't be here to protect my neck this time.

He would never, ever be coming home.

My daddy, Benny Rachpaul, had bought me these sneakers when I turned twelve over the summer. I wasn't about to let two older boys strolling down 125th Street snatch them off me.

Besides me being humiliated by it, my mother would whup my butt if she knew I had let some dudes swipe my shoes. And then, when he found out, Daddy Rachpaul would drive over and whup me again.

I flipped up the collar of my blue parka and continued down 125th Street, but rushed my step a little bit more. I heard the two boys following me quicken their pace. Their footsteps behind me crunched on the ice that much faster. My heart was beating faster too.

The streets around me were cheery, though. Harlem's main street was laid out tonight with bright lights, and Christmas tunes played constant on loudspeakers. I guess to put you more in the Christmas spirit.

But for me, there was nothing, and I mean nothing, that would ever make me feel Christmassy again. I was through with it.

Done.

Done with all of the Christmas music, wreaths, ornaments and happy holiday shoppers. I had decided weeks ago that I would never be happy again.

Because it wasn't fair.

Wasn't fair to get robbed of somebody I thought would be there for the rest of my life. Someone who was supposed to spend this Christmas with me, plus lots more Christmases!

It also wasn't fair that I couldn't even walk down 125th Street without being harassed. Rushing along down the sidewalk, I glanced up at all the men who were passing. All of them older and most of them Black like me. I was the youngest one out here and one of the few who felt scared to walk down this street.

For us young brothers, taking a stroll down here, even on Christmas Eve, was not relaxing at all. I felt like I had put my life on the line, straight up.

All of these old dudes lived in a different world from me.

I crossed the street and dipped into a gift shop on the corner. Grinning wide smiles, my two "buddies" waited for me outside, one of them sitting down on a fire hydrant and wiggling his fingers at me like I was a little infant in a stroller.

I sucked my teeth and turned toward the salesclerk.

"Happy holidays, my young man," the clerk said. "Help you find something?" For a minute, his eyes peeped outside at the two boys waiting. He frowned at them.

I watched them leave and sighed with relief. The clerk cocked his bald head to one side.

"I need a excellent Christmas gift," I said. "One for my mother, and another one for her, um, *friend*. And for my father. But I don't have much money."

"Last-minute shoppers," he said, smiling at me. "Come on. We'll get you straightened up. You're lucky we're open this late on Christmas Eve—125th Street is shutting down."

125th is a big street that runs from the East River on the east side of Manhattan to the Hudson River on the west side of Manhattan. The street cuts right through the neighborhood of Harlem and is where most of the main stores and shops and businesses are. The Apollo Theater, the Adam Clayton Powell Building and the Studio Museum are all lined up along 1-2-5. If Harlem was a human body, then 125th would be its pumping heart, throbbing all the time.

I don't know what the neighborhood's brain would be.

As I flew back toward home, I suddenly realized how heavy the gifts were that I had just bought in that shop. Ma and Yvonne would both be happy, I hoped. And Daddy, with his gift too.

But the bag handle cut into my fingers.

And just as I switched the plastic shopping bag to my other hand, I saw them. Across the wide blacktopped, slushy street, those two older boys had caught sight of me again. I started to step even faster down 125th Street, toward St. Nick, hoping I could make it to the border before they could catch me.

Where I live, it's all about borders.

And territories.

And crews.

When you're a little kid in Harlem, you can pretty much go anywhere and do anything as long as you're careful. But when you start to get old—about my age, twelve—things start to change.

You can't go everywhere.

You got to start worrying about crews. Crews are like cliques. Groups of mostly boys, and sometimes females, who hang out together. Mostly for fun, but for protection too.

And each crew got its territory in their neighborhood. And if you ain't from that hood, or a member of that set, you need to stay out.

When I was young, I used to have a friend over on East 127th Street. His name was Cody. We used to play boxball and dodgeball on East 127th all the time, even though I lived on the West Side.

Nowadays when I see Cody and he's with his crew, we don't talk at all. He just glares at me like I'm about to get jumped. He does it because we live in different places and we're old now.

That's how crews work.

So tonight, when I finally turned off of 125th and onto Eighth Av', the boys following me had to stop right there. There wasn't no real roadblock set up for them. If they had really wanted to, they could'a kept on following me, right up the block and straight into St. Nick projects.

But if they'd done that, somebody would'a jumped them boys.

Or worse.

"Yo, whattup, Lolly," Concrete said to me when I walked up the path into St. Nick. We slapped hands. "Lolly Rachpaul," he said again.

"Hey, 'Crete," I said to him. "How Day-Day?"

"He fine," Concrete said. "Thanks for asking. How your moms?"

"She fine," I said. "Merry Christmas!"

"Yo, man, I don't celebrate White Jesus Day no more!" he shouted. "This is the holiday of the Oppressor."

Concrete, about thirty, was ten years older than what Jermaine would'a been. 'Crete was what we called him. I didn't even know what his real name was, and he probably didn't know that my real name wasn't Lolly, which is what everybody called me.

"Sorry, man," I told him.

'Crete didn't even live in St. Nick, but he was always there, hanging around the big courtyard at its center. As far back as I remember, he had always been in that courtyard, peddling weed. He was a dealer, or "street pharmacist."

The place where I lived, the St. Nicholas Houses— otherwise known as the projects—was like a big family. Just like in a real family, you got some "relatives" you're cool with and others you can't stand, or who act up all the time.

St. Nick Houses was just like that.

It was home.

I got to my building, where I lived with my moms, walked in through the broken door and took the steps, because our elevator was jacked up too—the city didn't never fix nothing.

Seven flights of stairs!

About half the way up, the stairwell got all dark. The lights on this floor had burnt out, meaning I had to be careful climbing stairs in the gloominess.

Being in the dark forced my brain to concentrate more on the smell, which was mostly laid-over pee. You got used to it, though, the pee smell.

Just then, I raised one foot up and hit something. Something big and lumpy. The big lump jumped and clubbed my leg.

I stumbled back and almost tripped down the stairs, until I realized the big lump was Moses. Who was a old drunk man. When it was real cold outside, like it was tonight, he sometimes slept in the stairs.

Until the kids ran him out of here.

Or the cops.

"Merry Christmas, old drunk," I said to him.

"Show respect, boy!" he shouted after me. "I ain't no drunk. I only booze it up twice a year—"

"Yeah, I know, Moses: when it's your birthday and when it's *not* your birthday."

His jokes, I'd heard them all before.

Moses cackled like a old witch in the darkness while I continued climbing stairs.

2

I unlocked our front door and crept in.

Grabbing my shopping bag close to my chest, I snuck past Ma and Yvonne. They were busy cooking dinner for our Christmas Eve bash. I smelled Ma's famous roti and Yvonne's mac and cheese baking and that pointy smell of callaloo cooking on top of the stove.

Ma yelled out, "Lolly, you back?"

"Yeah!"

I shot straight for my bedroom and slammed the door.

· ✚ ✚ ✚ ·

One thing about me, I love Legos.

I may have been too old for them, but I had a million different Lego kits—space ones, dinosaurs, trucks and cars—all lining the walls of my bedroom on shelves. They used to get on Jermaine's nerves since I had so many of them, and me and him used to share our bedroom.

Now it's just me in here.

Every time I walk into our room, I have to face Jermaine's empty twin bed, sitting across from mine.

After getting the gift wrap out of my mother's bedroom, I plopped down on my bed and wrapped up the gifts I had just bought. Then I laid back and counted my Lego kits. Right now I had forty-six different ones, and tomorrow morning I would probably get some more.

I took pride in closely following the blueprints for each kit. Everything I built was *exactly* how it appeared on the box.

I shut my eyes.

Our front door buzzed.

Soon enough, I heard Ma answer it and caught her wishing Vega a merry Christmas. His loud Dominican voice boomed back: him and his family was flying to DR on Christmas Day tomorrow.

My mother tried to sound interested.

Vega always talked like he was outside. Which was weird because when he played his musical instrument, he was real calm and silent.

My eyes still shut, I heard him bounce in through my bedroom door and plop down on Jermaine's old bed. He was quiet for a minute, I guess analyzing me.

"You ain't sleep, nigga," I heard him say loudly.

I couldn't help laughing, so I opened my eyes.

"Whattup," he said, and then sang very sweetly: *"I'm dreaming of a Black Christmas."*

I laughed again. But my laughs had been weird lately. The good feeling that usually came with them only lasted a second. Then I fell right back to feeling all dark again.

Vega knew this. He was my best friend.

"You think your ma got you that smartphone you wanted?" he asked.

I shrugged and rolled over on my side. "She says it'd put me in danger." I pointed an imaginary gun at him and pulled the trigger. "She don't wanna paint a big target on her boy's chest."

"Yeah." Vega stood. He checked out the Rocky the Clown poster that hung on my wall. "You think Benny Rachpaul'll buy it for you?" he asked.

I shrugged again. "No telling with my daddy."

"Hey, is he rolling through tonight?"

"You know how he feel about Ma and her friends."

Vega nodded. "Yeah, but how long her and Yvonne been dating?"

"A long time," I answered.

Casimiro Vega lived one floor above me with his parents and little sister, Iris. They looked basically Black and you would think that they were until they opened their mouths to say something in Dominican, or Spanish.

His mother couldn't speak English too proper. They were all Dominicans with real dark skin.

My own skin wasn't as dark as Vega's. Mine was reddish brown and my cheekbones poked out a lot. I also had truly tiny eyes. I hated my eyes. They were almost slits.

I narrowed my eyes even more as Vega studied one of my Lego kits on a shelf.

He said, "I got a gay aunt, we just found out. She just told my mother at Thanksgiving." Vega picked up a city bus. I always got nervous when somebody handled my Legos. "But everybody knew already. She act just like a dude. Drives a big bus for the city. *Vroom!*"

"*Butch*," I said, describing how she acted.

"Yeah," Vega agreed. He started giggling and almost dropped my Lego model.

"Man!" I shouted. "Be careful."

"Ain't nobody gonna drop your stupid bus," he said, and put it back on the shelf. He pointed toward my bulletin board, with all my Lego blueprints. "I could draw better blueprints than these. They should hire me," he said.

"*Right.*" I sighed. "I hope Daddy does roll through for Christmas."

"You just want him to bring you that new phone!" Vega shouted, laughing.

I shook my head. "I just wanna see him."

And right then, our doorbell rang again. I knew it was

Daddy, and I jumped up to answer the door before Ma could. I thought that if she answered it and Daddy peeked in and saw her girlfriend in our kitchen cooking, he might turn right around and leave.

So I ran to our front door, but there wasn't nobody there but our neighbor Steve.

Now, I liked Steve Jenkins, don't get me wrong.

He was tall and light-skinned and lived with his moms right next door to us. Him and my brother, Jermaine, used to spend all their time together when they were little, like me and Vega, my mother said.

That all changed when they turned thirteen. Jermaine went in one direction—staying out more, running the streets—and Steve went another way, spending more time in after-school and art programs.

Now Jermaine was gone and Steve made movies.

Well, he didn't really make movies, but he recorded the sound for movies and TV shows. I wouldn't mind doing something like that when I'm twenty, working on movies. That'd be cool.

I turn thirteen next summer, so I got a minute.

Steve came back to my bedroom, where Vega was shaking the big Christmas gift that had been sitting on Jermaine's bed the past week—a gift that I had hoped had come from Jermaine. Even though my brother was gone, lately I had started thinking: what if it was all a trick?

What if my brother was hiding out somewhere? Like the supposedly dead rapper Tupac Shakur?

Maybe him and Tupac were really chilling somewhere together.

I smiled thinking about this.

Steve scoped out all of my new Lego kits I'd built since he was last over. He studied them like he was trying to give them a grade.

"You'd make a excellent architect, Lolly," he finally said. "You always follow your blueprints so *exact*."

"That's my thing," I said. "I like them to be just like the box."

Steve picked up the same bus that Vega had almost let fall. This time I didn't feel so nervous. I knew he wouldn't drop it.

"He needs to come up with something *new*, Steve," Vega said. "He should build a Lego zombie. With somebody's eyeballs and human brains dripping out of its mouth."

I sucked my teeth and held up one of my airplanes. It was dusty. I wished I had cleaned my kits off before Steve had seen them.

"You know *Casimiro* has a point," Steve said to me. He used Vega's first name, which he knew Vega hated.

"The only point *Casimiro* has is on the top of his head," I said. I watched Vega's face for him to react. He was frowning, but trying not to giggle.

"Not about that zombie garbage, Loll. But about you making something new," Steve said. He dropped onto the bed next to Vega. "Not many of us have rich imaginations, but you do. It's hard for most people to come up with any original ideas. Everybody consumes the same old TV shows, pix and memes over and over, regurgitating the same old ideas over and over."

"Regurgitating?" Vega asked.

"Puking back up what you already ate," I said.

"Oh," said Vega. "Like zombies puking up brains."

Steve went on, "If you only expose yourself to whatever everybody else does, you'll never create anything new. I think that's what got your brother: He couldn't see any other way out of here besides *dealing*. Got caught up in that street lifestyle, like that sheisty Rockit and all them."

He reached into the plastic bag he'd been carrying and flung me and Vega each a wrapped gift. I could tell they were books by the way they felt. Vega had thought the same thing, by the disappointed look on his face.

"Casimiro, I brought your gift over here because I figured you'd be with your man," Steve said. "Cheering him up."

"Quit calling me Casimiro," Vega said, tearing open his gift. It was a paperback. One on violin technique for kids. This was a book Vega would actually read, I knew. He had been playing an instrument ever since the fourth grade, when his mother enrolled him in music class.

My book was all about buildings and stuff. *A Pattern of Architecture*. It was a giant hardback filled with pictures of stuff famous architects had built from all over the world.

It was funny because it wasn't something that I would'a thought to ask for, but sitting there then in my room, it seemed like something I had been wanting. I just hadn't known that I had wanted it.

3

I wanted everybody to go home.

Steve had left a while ago, but now Ma's friend Mr. Jonathan and his family had come over to celebrate the holiday. I just wasn't feeling them.

"That all the pastelles you want, sugar?" Ma asked me.

"Shovel some more of my mac and cheese on your plate, Loll," Yvonne added in. "That's lush. Three cheeses. Put some hair on that frail little chest of yours!" Yvonne snickered.

Ma said, "I don't know where Sugar got that lil' chest from. His father's chest is broad." Yvonne went on laughing. Ma's face was blank.

I ignored them and continued stuffing three plates with food for the other kids.

I heard Mr. Jonathan call out from the living room, "Will you two lesbians stop harassing my friend Wallace! He is a twelve-year-old boy with a twelve-year-old boy's chest! Not like you two balloon-bosom Weather Girls!"

Yvonne burst out laughing again.

Our apartment hadn't heard lots of laughter over the past two months. Hearing it now reminded me of how things used to be when Jermaine was still here.

I watched Ma search through cans of soda in the fridge. She had a dejected look on her smooth, coffee-colored face. My mother was a pretty normal mom, but different at the same time.

The thing that was the most normal about her was that she loved reading mysteries. Something different was that she collected Pez candies. Not like the actual candy, but more the little dispensers that come with the candy.

Ma had a huge collection of these Pez containers in our apartment. She had built special shelves and cabinets to hold them all. I guessed she owned over three hundred of them things. I think Ma expected me to take over her collection eventually, but I'm not interested.

Ma worked as a security guard in Downtown Brooklyn.

I think she got the job because she was so intimidating. Not that tall, but just really big. Both her and Yvonne were built like New York Giants linemen. But they both were harmless. They'd usually prefer to joke before they would tackle anybody.

"Don't make me march in there to defend my Wallace!" I heard Mr. Jonathan shout out again.

"Shut up, Jonathan!" Yvonne shouted back.

Even though Mr. Jonathan was a man, he really acted more like an auntie to me. He was a work friend of Ma's who had known her since the old days—back when she was still with my father. In fact, I knew that my daddy blamed Mr. Jonathan for making my mother gay.

"Dat limp-wrist friend of your mum still hang about?" Daddy would ask me whenever I saw him. When I would say yes, then Daddy would go on and on and on and on about how that Mr. Jonathan had been jealous of him and Ma's joy and had convinced her that she liked women, when she really didn't.

I wasn't even sure how that worked. Could you really make somebody gay just by chatting with them?

I hoped that I wouldn't turn out that way, because I talked to a lot of gays. I actually do like them, but they got too much *drama* to deal with. So many people hate them and call them names that I don't think it's something anybody would really pick to be if they had a choice in it. Who would choose to be gay when they knew it was so much easier to be straight?

I steadied the three dishes in my arms and started to leave our kitchen when Ma slid a can of fruit-punch soda under my left arm. She suddenly hugged me really tight; I thought I was gonna drop everything.

"Give that soda to Jonathan," Ma said. "My cherry cobbler's almost done."

"I don't feel like nothing," I said.

"I know, I know," she said, unhappy.

Yvonne teased, "Lolly got all that grub in his hands and ain't hungry?"

Ma said to me, "But at least you got to test my cobbler for me, honey. My blood sugar's probably sky-high already."

I nodded. I had only grabbed this food to make them think I was really starved. I hadn't wanted Ma and Yvonne to nag me again, about not eating so much lately.

My mother peeked into the oven with a firm, miserable aspect on her face. It was the first Christmas after Jermaine. I wondered if every Christmas from now on would feel this sorry.

I hurried out of the kitchen and passed into our living room, balancing the plates. Mr. Jonathan relaxed in a chair there, gazing at our little Christmas tree with its twinkly lights.

He was a older dude with black-and-gray hair on top of his head, mixed together. His eyes always sparkled like he had glitter in them. Mr. Jonathan pulled the can of soda from under my arm.

"Don't you let them get to you, Wallace," Mr. Jonathan said. "You are entirely normal for your age."

I shrugged.

"You okay?" he asked. "You been so *down* lately. You and your mother, slinking around here just as despondent..."

I squinted at him.

"Despondent," he said again. *"Sad."*

"Oh, okay."

Mr. Jonathan shook his gray head. He missed Jermaine too. "You tell Markka and Darius not to make a mess back there with all that food!"

"Your father said not to make a mess," I told the two kids sitting on my rug. I gave one plate to the girl, Markka, one plate to her brother, Darius, and the last one to Vega, still lying across Jermaine's bed.

My bedroom was crowded.

Out in the living room, I heard music. Ma had started playing her old chutney and calypso tunes. Harry Belafonte singing "Mary's Boy Child" drifted in from the living room. I shut my bedroom door.

No more Christmas.

"Pastelles!" Vega said, smiling into his plate. He noticed I didn't have one. "Where's yours?"

"I ain't hungry," I said. "I'm waiting on Ma's cherry cobbler, anyhow."

Vega sat up on the bed and looked down at Markka. "Yo, his ma make the best pastelles!"

"Not as good as Jermaine used to make 'em," I said.

Ma's pastelles were just all right. I didn't know what

Vega was ranting about. Jermaine's were so good because he learned how from our grandmother. When she used to babysit him, before she cut Ma off.

"Pastelles," Markka said, making a depressed face. She sniffed Vega's plate, frowned a little and said, "Sorry, I don't eat pig."

I don't think I had ever seen Markka really happy.

Mr. Jonathan had adopted both her and her brother out of foster care. The two of them were genuine brother and sister, and Ma said Mr. Jonathan had wanted to keep them together as a family.

"She's allergic," her brother, Darius, added. "Pork."

How could you be allergic to pork?

Darius jammed a spoonful of Yvonne's mac and cheese in his mouth. His eyes were glued to the news on my TV. Supposedly, Santa was coming tonight, the TV weatherman lied to us.

"You got roaches," Darius said, pointing toward my closet. "I saw one."

"Everybody got bugs, dummy!" Vega said to him. "Yo, Lolly! When you gonna open up this Christmas present? I wanna know what's inside."

"Who gave you that giant present?" Darius asked, shifting his eyes to the gift.

"A notorious gangsta!" Vega called out. Markka's gaze went to Vega and then to me, but she didn't say nothing.

"This dude named Rockit gave it to me," I told her. "But I think it's from my brother. He used to run with him."

"Your brother that got shot?" she asked.

"That's the only brother he got, stupid," Vega said to her. "Yo, Loll, I bet Rockit gave you a box full of drugs." He shook the present. "Or a Glock!"

Darius turned full around now to peek at the gift. He had macaroni and cheese dripping from his mouth. "You got a gun in there?" he asked. His voice choked from too much food.

"Vega, I told you I think it's from Jermaine," I said. "And he wouldn't give me no gun."

He ran across the room with the gift and landed on top of me, crushing my bones. "Prove it!" Vega screamed.

I felt like banging him in his face.

I was hating all of the Christmas cooking and tunes and dumb holiday specials . . . but this one Christmas gift had slowly grabbed hold of something inside of me.

I had been kind of curious ever since Rockit had dropped it off for me about a week ago. I had been coming home from playing ball when I heard somebody call out my name.

"Yo, Lolly!" the voice yelled. "Lolly Rachpaul! Come here, negro!"

And it was Rockit, a friend of my brother's from before.

Rockit was sitting on the passenger side of this monster SUV—*bananas*—right on the street in front of St. Nick. One of his boys sat behind the wheel. This enormous black-and-white dog watched me from the backseat, like it was trying to figure out who, or what, I was.

"Where you been at, man?" said Rockit. "Me and my boy CJ been waitin' on you since *three*, man."

"You should'a come over to the rec center, Rock," I said. "I been hooping. Is that your dog? He's a pit mix, right?"

"That's my boy's," he said. "His name Diesel. Go pet him. He's a friendly pup."

I reached in through the open window and scratched Diesel on the middle of his head. The dog closed his eyes and laid back his ears.

Rockit went on, "Your boy Concrete said you had stepped out. Here, man." Then he shoved the red-and-white, candy-cane-striped present through the SUV's window. I eyed his gift, not grabbing it. "I didn't wanna leave it with your moms. You know how she get."

I nodded.

"Take it, little man! 'Maine wanted you to have this."

I grabbed the present then, turning it around in my hands.

"You all right?" Rockit asked. "You know if you ever need anything, you just reach out, okay? If anybody ever bother you . . ." He gave me his number on the back of an old receipt. I knew Ma would be heated about that.

His friend behind the wheel spoke up without taking his eyes off his phone. "We gotta roll, Rock," he said. "DeMarion's waiting on us in the Boogie Down."

Ignoring him, Rockit went on to me, "Me and Jermaine was like brothers. So that make me and you brothers. *A'ight?*"

I nodded. He grinned.

"I ain't never had no little brother before," Rockit said.

"Yo, *Rock*—" his friend started again.

"*Chill, Corey!*" Rockit snapped at him. "You see I'm being Santa here!"

"Wallace!" somebody shouted. As soon as I heard that voice, my whole body froze up. I glanced behind me and saw Ma on the footpath, clomping toward me and Rockit.

Her face was all frowned up. She stopped at the SUV and glared at Rockit, the dog, me and then the candy-cane gift in my hands. Ma grabbed her hip and dove in.

"I know this ain't Calvin Bridgewater bearing gifts for my son."

"Hello, Ms. Rachpaul—" Rockit answered.

"Don't come around here talking to my boy. I will call the cops, yuh hear? Lolly, cut upstairs!"

I started to leave, but she yanked the present out of my hand. As I hiked down the path toward our building, I could hear her and Rockit go at it.

"You still blaming me for what happened to 'Maine," he said to her.

"You had a foul influence on my son!" she shouted. "You and that barbershop! Jermaine wasn't nothing like that before. He was *good*!"

And the two of them went at it like that for ten minutes. Rockit kept repeating that even though Ma hated him, my brother Jermaine had wanted me to have this present. That's the only reason she kept it and why I was about to open it now.

The main thing I had hoped for was that under this bright wrapping paper there would be a letter from Jermaine. Or some secret note from him maybe. A note confessing to me that he was still around. That for some reason he had had to fake everything and go undercover.

Here in my bedroom, Vega, Markka and Darius gathered around and I ripped off the red-and-white wrapping paper, my heart thumping hard.

Inside was one of the new video game console units. The latest model. I had seen one online for over four hundred dollars.

Vega whistled.

I looked all around for my letter, my note, but there wasn't one. This console felt like it was a gift for another kid.

I wasn't even into video games.

What did Rockit mean that Jermaine had wanted me to have a video game console?

Vega's ma called him back upstairs. They had to get ready to fly away to the Dominican Republic the next day. He left, upset that he didn't even get a chance to play with my new system and that he would have to wait two weeks before he could.

For the rest of the night, me, Markka and Darius played the one video game that came free with the console. After they had left, I tried playing some more, but I was just not into it.

Instead, I grabbed some cherry cobbler and opened the big book on architecture that my neighbor Steve had gave me. My fingers flicked through the pages of *A Pattern of Architecture*.

And then, just after midnight, I went kinda nuts. Like, I got this go-go sort of energy.

About ten of my Lego kits came down off my shelves. I threw them to the ground and tugged them all apart, dumping the pieces into a pile. I faced all my other Lego kits—all neat and tidy on my shelves—and decided to do the same.

I jerked and hauled them all down like a maniac.

I wasn't sure if it was just the sugar from the cherry cobbler or if it was bottled-up stuff over Jermaine or if maybe I had just stayed up too late.

But something had grabbed on to me.

I didn't know what, but it gave me crazy energy to want to rip apart all of my Legos and make them into something else.

Something different.

4

L ate the next morning I was sitting on our couch and setting up the new phone I had just got.

After I had got it to work, my mother and me sat at the kitchen table eating cornflakes with milk and cheese danish. Ma always liked having cheese danish on Christmas morning. She bought them from the Fairway supermarket because she said they had the freshest.

"Thanks again for the new phone, Ma," I told her.

"You are welcome, sugar," she said. Ma suddenly looked at me all serious. "Be careful out there with that phone, Wallace. Watch your back. Do not use it in the streets for the whole hood to see."

I nodded and started downloading.

She said, "And don't be strutting around here telling everybody you got that new fancy game console. That's the last thing we need, them breaking in here to steal it and getting away with my Pez collection."

I nodded. I really didn't think they would want Ma's Pez

holders, but I kept that to myself. This Harlem free Wi-Fi was *sooo* slow for downloads. I guess that's why it was free.

"I shouldn't let you keep that console," Ma said. She shoved half a danish in her mouth.

I nodded again, checking out what was online with my phone.

Ma went on, "I don't know why I . . . I just don't . . ." Her head slunk down toward the table. Out of nowhere, she had started sobbing again.

I remembered even Daddy had cried like a little kid the last time he was over here. Couldn't help it. I stood over Ma and held on, hugging her from behind, letting my chin rest on the top of her head.

Her scalp smelled nice. Like the olive oil she used to condition her hair.

I stood there holding her for a few minutes while she cried herself out. I asked, "You think Daddy'll come over today?"

Ma sat up straight, clutching my hand. She wiped her eyes with her other hand and started sifting through her cornflakes.

"You think he'll come for Christmas?" I went on.

"*Well,*" she started with a sigh, "you know Benjamin as well as I do. Your father makes up his own mind, his kind of way. If he'd been around more, maybe Jermaine would'a turned out different."

"Daddy comes around sometimes."

She grunted and squeezed my hand tighter.

"I turned out okay," I said. "You're the best moms. And father too."

She laughed out loud at this, kissed the back of my hand and let it go. "I just worry," Ma said.

My phone's screen flashed and chirped. Vega had just sent me another message, telling me he had got some new boots for Christmas. Earlier, his first message had read: "Welcome to the 21st century, sucka!"

Just now another message said that him and his family were trying to leave for the airport. They were all still upstairs, running late as usual, and his father had started screaming at his mother, blaming everything on her.

His little sister, Iris, had started to cry.

I shook my head, surprised that I couldn't hear all of them yelling from down here. Just then, the door buzzer buzzed.

Ma smiled at me. "You ain't going to answer that door? You never know, that might be Santa. He might have forgot something last night."

"Unpossible. Santa don't come to the PJs," I said. "Even if this *is* named St. Nick."

But Daddy comes to the PJs, I suddenly thought. I ran and swung open our front door.

Yvonne.

She held two big ol' black trash bags.

I guess my face had seemed dejected, because after Yvonne took one look at me, she went, "Well, merry friggin' Christmas to you too!"

I sucked my teeth and stepped aside to let her in. She slouched through our front door, dragging her sloppy trash bags behind her. They left wet trails on the floor. I frowned.

Yvonne, Ma's girlfriend for years, was a custodian at Tuttle's Toy Emporium at Rockefeller Center downtown. She swept up the store and hauled out the trash.

Like Mr. Jonathan, she acted like my auntie. She wore her hair dyed blond and in a Mohawk and loved to treat me, my mother and even Vega to dinners at Applebee's.

"*Um,*" I started, "why'd you bring your trash over here?"

I noticed she was way out of breath. I guessed it was from dragging these two huge plastic bags up the seven flights to our place.

Ma came racing out of the kitchen. She stopped in front of me and Yvonne. Ma's mouth was hanging open and she was staring at us, like she expected somebody to pull a rabbit out of a hat.

Yvonne said to me, "Lolly, I am not sure that you deserve me hauling all this *yick-yack* through the snow and up seven floors, but I love you like my own blood, so . . ." She laughed at Ma, then emptied up one of the trash bags, pouring it out all over our living room floor.

I hopped back, not wanting to let any of that crap attack my new house slippers. But then I noticed something strange. It really wasn't trash at all.

"Merry Christmas, Lolly!" Yvonne yelled.

They were Legos!

Millions and millions of Legos.

"This other one is full of them too," Yvonne shouted, pointing toward the second trash bag.

I was so stunned I couldn't say *nothing*. I knelt down and poured my hands through the mountain of plastic pieces on our floor. This mountain was even bigger than the one I had made last night when I yanked apart all my Lego kits.

These bricks, added to the secret project I had started in my room last night, might really add up to something. There was lots I could do. . . .

Ma smiled at me. "What you think, Lolly?"

"I got them all from my job," Yvonne said. "They were gonna pitch 'em all out in the scrap, but I was like, 'Wait a minute. I know somebody who could *use* these!'" She bent over laughing.

I waded my hands through all the Legos some more. There were so many. They made a sound like money, like quarters tumbling together.

"What do you *think*, Lolly?" Ma said again.

The thing was, I couldn't!

Man, I just *couldn't*!

5

M e and Vega inched down the icy front steps of our middle school. I still didn't believe that winter break was already over and I was back in class again. The two weeks off sure seemed like nothing now.

It was brick cold out this January afternoon. Vega was wearing the new shiny black parka that his grandma in DR had given him for Three Kings.

Vega had told me that in the Dominican Republic, Three Kings' Day was actually a bigger holiday than Christmas Day. Or at least as big.

Before the little kids in DR would go to bed the night before Three Kings, they would leave small boxes of grass underneath their beds. The grass was meant to feed the camels that the three wise men would be riding. The next morning the kids would wake up to find a bunch of presents loaded at the foot of their beds.

So for them, it was like having two Christmases every

year. I remember thinking that wasn't fair and I had asked my mother if they had Three Kings' Day in Trinidad.

Though my moms called herself Trini, for Trinidadian, she had never even been to Trinidad and Tobago in the Caribbean. Her parents had been born there. But ever since my grandma found out her daughter had started dating women, she didn't speak to Ma too much.

"Mr. Ali wanna talk to you," Vega said. "I ran into him before school. You do something?"

I supposed I knew what Mr. Ali wanted to talk about. But I wasn't looking forward to it. Ali scared me sometimes.

"How's your violin, Vega?" I asked, not wanting to talk about Mr. Ali.

Vega and I had to cut to the middle of the street. All the kids were hanging so deep in front of our school that we couldn't move on the sidewalk.

"Ms. D. says I'm coming along," Vega answered.

He had been playing since he was nine. He wasn't that bad. I didn't think anybody was expecting him to play violin in nobody's orchestra anytime, but listening to him didn't make your ears bleed.

"Watch out!" Vega called to me in the street. He held me back.

This girl Tisha shouted like somebody had cut her and ran in front of us. She stopped hard and grabbed the sleeve of Vega's new coat to keep from falling. He jerked his sleeve away from her.

Another boy, Freddy, came chasing after Tisha. He bear-hugged her and they both slumped to the street, laughing.

Me and Vega stepped over them.

I almost kicked them instead. I had been so mean lately.

"I can't believe she yanked my new coat," Vega said, examining it for damage. "I was only gonna wear it around our place. Or on special occasions. But then I thought that'd be stupid."

"Yeah. That *would* be stupid. How would you only wear a parka inside your apartment?"

"Shut up."

We started back toward West 127th Street, toward after-school.

And Mr. Ali.

The funny thing about Mr. Ali was his face. His face was weird.

On one side of it, it just kind of got out of balance. The left side of his face was normal; his right side kind of seemed like somebody had smashed his skull with a hammer and put the pieces back together again. Only the pieces had not fit right.

Me and Vega walked quiet for a while until he asked me again about my *castle*. Besides my mother and Yvonne, he was the only one I had told about it. But I still hadn't let him come down to our apartment to inspect it.

"Loll, man, why won't you let me see this secret *project* you built?" he asked.

I shrugged.

"You must be embarrassed about it," he said.

I didn't respond because I knew Vega was only saying that to try to trick me into showing him. Ever since Yvonne had given me all those Legos for Christmas, I had been building.

I had started in my bedroom. Then that got too small. I moved what I had been building into the living room and it got even bigger.

Ma had loved my castle when it stayed in my bedroom. After I moved it, she started to grumble.

And Ma was losing patience with it taking up so much space. It was a good thing that ever since Jermaine had gone, she had let me get away with more stuff that I didn't used to get away with. Lots of times, I only needed to serve up a sad face and she would back down.

Vega and me crossed over 125th Street.

"They following us," Vega said to me, dipping his head behind mine. I tracked where his skullcap had pointed, and I saw those same two older boys that had been following me on Christmas Eve.

"They from East 127th," Vega said. "They been stressing my cousin to join they set."

"That would make you and your cousin enemies."

Vega used his gloves to wipe his nose. "Let's *move*," he said, and we took off running toward after-school before the two older boys could catch us.

· ✛ ✛ ✛ ·

"Shut your pothole face, *nappy*," Sunnshyne said, whispering at Vega.

"Moonshyne!" Vega whispered back to Sunny. She glared at him.

Every afternoon at after-school these two went at it like this. Sunnshyne would make fun of Vega's knotted-up hair, and he would tease about how dark-skinned she was. And I had to sit right in the middle of it.

Our after-school program was for St. Nick residents and those who lived in the hood. It was located in the community center, on the far side of the projects, about as far away from my building as you could get and still be in my development.

It was mostly about forcing us to do our homework, and getting help studying. But we sometimes did fun things like go on trips or learn to make things like homemade windmills or different types of recipes.

I had been coming to the St. Nick after-school for

years. It was probably why Vega and me had become best friends.

Today Ms. Jenna had just finished showing us how to make fresh hummus from scratch using olive oil and garlic and cans of chickpeas. Most of the time at after-school we studied and learned things, but sometimes they gave us classes on how to be more healthy.

To me, hummus in my mouth didn't taste too healthy at all. None of the kids thought it did except for Darrell Buckney, who was crazy anyhow. He was a fat boy with a mustache and on some kind of meds.

Ms. Jenna thought her hummus tasted good. She was our main after-school instructor. For somebody white from Ohio, she had a big butt.

When she strolled up here every day along Frederick Douglass Boulevard from the A train, Ms. Jenna would get all kinds of shouts and whistles from dudes wanting to hit her up because of her big butt.

It disgusted her, she said.

"Vega, you smell like the subway," Sunny whispered.

"Not every subway stinks, *mammal*," he whispered back.

"Yeah, but we're *all* mammals, dummy," she said.

Sunnshyne Dixon-Knight, or Sunny, wasn't bad-looking, but her attitude made her ugly. She was tall for a girl and usually wore her head in braids. She had dark, smooth skin that looked like it was carved out of midnight.

Vega pretended like he was about to pop her. Sunny dared him, lifting her chin.

"Nappy!" she whispered at him.

My best friend's hair *was* like a bush of thick black wires. It was almost like Vega's body grew so much hair his head didn't know what to do with it. I think he grew at least an inch of hair every night when he slept.

"You better not touch me, Vega," Sunny warned. "Lolly'll punch you in the neck if you do." She smiled at me.

"Everyone, I have to step out for a moment," Ms. Jen told us kids. "Start your homework. I'm just down the hall." Before she left, she scowled at us as if to say there would be problems if we acted up while she was gone. We all got the message.

Well, most of us did.

After a couple of minutes of us studying in peace, Darrell Buckney said, "*Ugh!* It smells like balls in here." We all laughed.

"I told you, you *stank*," Sunny told Vega.

Then Quintesha Charles said, "Somebody farted."

Why did Quintesha have to say that?

Darrell B. flew up out of his seat and started sniffing at everybody's butts to see who had farted.

"Hey! Hey!" Vega shouted at him. "Leave my *bumpay* alone!"

Everybody laughed some more, but when Darrell B. had

got to my seat and was standing behind me about to sniff my butt, I stood up and slung my pencil at him.

Of course, right when I threw my pencil was when Ms. Jenna had decided to stroll back inside the study room.

"Ms. Jen! He tried to smell my booty!" I shouted.

She stared at Darrell. Ms. Jen asked him, "Should I recommend they put you back on your medication, young man?" He looked ashamed after hearing this. I felt a little sorry for him.

Anyway, so she embarrassed him and I still got yelled at for hurling my pencil. Darrell B. just giggled in that weird kind of way he did. Like a wild hyena.

Ms. Jenna said, "Lolly, Mr. Ali wants to see you in his office."

My stomach gurgled. Everybody in the room gave me a look. Darrell B. laughed.

"Cut it out," Ms. Jenna told him. Then she said to me, "Mr. Ali wants..." She didn't finish. "Well, let's just go see him, hon."

6

"So I hear you're launching projectiles now," he said.

"Excuse me?" I said.

"You shot your pencil at one of my after-schoolers, Mr. Rachpaul," Mr. Ali went on. "That's what Lady Bug just said." Lady Bug is what Mr. Ali called Ms. Jenna.

I sighed. "Look, it wasn't even like that, man—"

"Excuse *you*, young man?"

"I mean, mister, uh, *sir*. Darrell B. was being Darrell B. That's all it was. I didn't do nothing."

Mr. Ali leaned back in his swivel chair. His bald brown head bounced against the wall behind him. He did that a lot. You could tell because the white wall had turned gray right where he had just tapped his head.

"He farted and tried to blame it on somebody else," I told Ali. He stared at me. I glanced at one of the plaques hanging above him on the wall. This one read: AKIL S. ALI, LSW. LSW meant Licensed Social Worker, I knew.

Though he was the center director, or boss, here, he didn't have no big office or nothing. I didn't like that it was so tight in here.

Mr. Ali was all right, I guess, but he nerve-wracked me sometimes. He was always trying to get into everybody's business.

"That's not the only thing with you," he said. "I've noticed a change. Lady Bug also said you've been sulky in class the past couple months, *despondent*."

"Ms. Jenna said what?"

Ali nodded. "'Despondent' only means—"

"*Sad*," I said.

"Yeah," Ali said. "Sad. Look, Lolly, I realize what happened to Jermaine is fairly recent. Just this past fall..."

I stopped listening.

In my mind, I saw Jermaine's bed. It looked like he was laying beneath the white covers. Only, the vision I saw was made out of Legos. I could see his hand peeking out from beneath the sheets. It was a brown hand, all blocky from being made out of Lego bricks.

I shook my head to wake from my daydream.

Mr. Ali had just finished saying a bunch of stuff I hadn't even heard.

He looked like he wanted me to respond.

"Every time I come home," I said out of nowhere, "and

see his bed in the corner, I expect to see him lying there. With his back facing me. And him grumbling for me to shut our door so Ma won't come in."

I looked down.

"It may be time to move out his bed," Ali said.

"I don't want that," I said, glaring at him. "Ma don't want that neither! It's his bed!"

"*His* bed?"

I felt stupid all of a sudden.

He leaned toward me. "Wallace, Jermaine doesn't need that bed any longer. He's *dead*—"

Hearing this made my knee jerk. I kicked the metal front of Ali's olive-green desk so hard that I left a dent in it. The desk shook and some manila folders fell to the floor. Ali sighed and leaned over to pick them up.

We didn't say nothing for a while.

"I'm sorry," I finally said.

He shrugged. "Let's have another talk next week."

I stood up, snatching my backpack off the floor.

"He's not coming back, Lolly," Mr. Ali said before I could leave. He spoke very quiet. "You need to accept it. It may sound callous, cold-blooded, but you will never see Jermaine again. At least, not in this life."

Ma had picked the coldest day in January for us to go skating, I swore.

I wasn't in a good mood because me and my moms had been arguing lately about my Lego castle. She had been complaining about it taking up so much room.

Right now I really wanted to be back at the crib, working on it, instead of tromping through the middle of Central Park in the wet snow.

I kicked a ball of ice against one of the gazillions of trees here. This park had more trees, streams, hills, bridges and footpaths than it knew what to do with.

Central Park was okay, but building my castle soothed my nerves. I really hadn't liked talking to Mr. Ali the other day in his office. I didn't like thinking about the stuff he was trying to make me think about. It dug up too much dirt.

And made me remember about how I had let Jermaine down.

I watched Ma and Yvonne walk ahead of me in the park, holding hands. Ma was dressed in a big puffy coat with work boots. Pieces of Yvonne's bright Mohawk stuck out from under her skullcap.

I wished I could lose both them and Mr. Ali from out of my life.

· + + + ·

At Wollman Rink Ma got us all inside for only five dollars apiece with a special coupon she had.

I didn't think that I would want to at first, but I really did ice-skate a lot. Maybe this had been an okay idea after all. It reminded me of when we used to come here as a family around the holidays.

While I took a break off the ice and ate a hot dog from the food hut, I leaned against the rail and watched Ma and Yvonne out there, skating around the rink. Ma was steady on her feet, but Yvonne was miserable.

She had never even been on the ice.

Yvonne had to hold on to Ma or the side rails or she would'a fell flat on her butt. She did a lot of that too. My mother was trying to teach Yvonne how to skate on her own when Yvonne lost her balance and yanked Ma down onto the ice with her.

The two of them sat there, laughing, trying to stand back up.

I tried to grin, but couldn't.

Even if it was funny to watch, seeing them two out there, trying to stand up together on that ice.

My after-school at the St. Nick community center would sometimes take us on skate outings to Wollman Rink. It was always a big deal, and at least a dozen kids would get yelled at for acting up on those trips.

Darrell Buckney was always one of them.

We had Darrell Buckney and also a Daryl Reynolds. Though their first names were spelled different, you said them just the same.

Ms. Jen had been confused when she had started here. She even tried to tell Darrell that based on how his name was spelled, it should actually be pronounced different than Daryl's name. Darrell's mother wasn't happy that Lady Bug had been trying to convince Darrell that his name wasn't right, so she stomped down here and cursed out Ms. Jen in front of the whole class.

After that we all said Darrell's name like his ma wanted us to.

Ms. Jen started calling them Darrell B. or Daryl R. to tell them apart.

The center was okay, but I didn't really like having Mr. Ali call me into his office to talk about my brother. It seemed like he was only trying to make me feel worse.

But a week after our first talk, here I was again, sitting across from his ugly face in his office. I tried to fix my eyeballs on something else to distract me. I sighed and read another one of his wall plaques to myself.

"That's from City College," Ali said, pointing at the

plaque I was eyeing. "I got my MS in psychotherapy there. *Way* back." He laughed, but I didn't find anything funny. "I trained in counseling *youth* in particular."

I squinted at him. I was beginning to wonder if I should trust him as much as I had been.

"You got kind of excited the last time you were in here," Ali said.

"Not really," I said.

"Oh yeah?" He pointed at the front of his old desk. "That dent ain't coming out, brother. Trashing up my furniture . . ."

I looked away. Mr. Ali grinned, all crooked.

"You got very angry, sir." He pulled out a desk drawer and offered me some gum. I declined. "I used to be angry like that. You gotta deal with anger, or anger will deal with you." Ali pointed at his face and grinned some more. He shoved a stick of gum into his mouth.

I watched him chew. "Your face, you mean?" I asked.

"Apert syndrome," Mr. Ali answered. "Type of birth defect. When I was younger, about your age, I used to be angry. At my father in particular."

I nodded, but didn't know what he meant.

"Why are you so angry?" Mr. Ali asked. "I understand how much you miss Jermaine. But are you mad at him?"

"No!" I shouted. *"Man . . ."*

Hearing him say that made me boil. But I tried to control myself this time. I stuffed it back down inside of me.

And I forced a smile.

"I *loved* my brother," I told him.

Ali looked suspicious.

"Jermaine was the only person I could talk to in the world and not have to use words," I said. "Sometimes, if we were walking down the street and somebody crazy would walk by or something funny would happen, me and Jermaine wouldn't have to say nothing to one another. Just one look and he knew exactly how I was thinking."

Remembering this made me feel even worse. I hated coming here.

Mr. Ali leaned back in his swivel chair and bumped his head against his wall. He stared at the ceiling, then closed his eyes.

"Deal with these emotions, Mr. Rachpaul," he said. "If we don't distinguish our heartache—don't at least attempt to work through it, you understand—it tends to pop up later. In different ways, *aberrant* ways." He frowned. "This gum is stale."

The metal trash can gonged as he spat the gum inside.

"Aberrant," he said again. "Bad behavior, bad things, man. So you're not gonna tell me who—or what—you're mad at?"

I thought about what I had done to Jermaine. I hadn't told anybody what had gone down between us before he had died. It upset my stomach thinking about it.

And yeah—it was bad.

7

The House of Moneekrom had devoured most of the living room. That was what I had named my Lego castle. I was afraid Ma was gonna blow up and make me tear it down any day now.

She'd better not. This was one of the best things I'd ever done.

Working on it made me feel better than any stupid talk with Mr. Ali.

Moneekrom was made up of all different colors of blocks, stacked right beside one another like rainbow walls. I had built round turrets all along the walls. And there were little arched bridges coming out of three sides of the castle.

In the center on top I had started building a huge dome that would cover the king's throne. As I built, I made up stories.

I had decided that it was where the aliens King Blaze and Queen Misteria lived. They had a son too. His name was Prince Stellar.

The House of Moneekrom had been handed down from one member of the Moneekrom family to the next. For over thousands of years, it had. And every time a new king was crowned, they added on a new wing to the alien castle, which was why I had to build it so enormous.

But over those thousands of years none of the Moneekrom kings or queens had been able to solve one big problem. . . .

I needed to write all this down somewhere.

Just then, I heard keys jingling in the front door and Ma came slumping in from work. She eyed me while hanging up her coat. I knew then she was about to start in again. I tensed my shoulders and started rearranging blocks on one of the castle's towers.

Her eyes sizzled the rear of my neck.

"You know I tripped over your lil' buildings last night?" she told the back of my head.

"I know," I said. "It took me an hour to fix your damage."

I heard her suck her teeth. My mother could slurp her teeth louder than anybody I knew. I kept working on my castle tower.

"Sugar," she started, "your buildings—"

"*House of Moneekrom*, Ma."

"Right," she said. "Mo-nee-krom needs to come down. It's took over the whole *blangdang* room. And I ain't tripping over it again. You can't see?"

I didn't say nothing. She sighed and stamped into her bedroom.

"Take it down, Wallace!" I heard her yell. "Or *I'll* take it down!"

She slammed her bedroom door.

"Daddy!" I shouted, and hugged him before he could even step through our doorway.

He laughed. "How is my warrior?" Daddy asked me.

"Good," I said.

"Here you go," he said, and tossed me a gift wrapped in snowflake Christmas paper.

"Late Christmas?" I asked him, and grinned.

"Late Christmas!" he answered.

Late Christmas was a holiday that only me and my father celebrated. The date changed every year. It happened on the day that he finally rolled through to give me my holiday gifts.

Though this year I was disappointed that it was only one gift. Usually the old dude came through with lots of them for me and at least one for Ma.

I tore open my present with him still standing in the doorway. It was a computer tablet with a wireless mouse. I liked it, but wasn't as excited as I guess I should'a been.

"Uh, Sir Wallace, sir, may we come indoors?" Daddy asked me, looking exasperated.

Just then, I realized two things: I had been blocking his way into our apartment, and he had somebody with him, what he called his *doux-doux*, or new girlfriend.

Her name was Heike and she was a funny-looking white German lady. My father could'a done better. He was a handsome man, even if he was old; he was almost forty.

People said I resembled him. We had the same curvy hair and noses with high bridges. I hoped I would get as diesel as he was. But doing construction helped him stay in shape.

"Wallace," he would say to me, "never couch at home watching TV when you could be doing something fruitful. Get out, boy. Jog. Go to the gym! Lift a barbell!"

Suddenly Ma shoved me to the side so Daddy and his girl could step in. I almost fell over. Ma didn't need to lift no barbells.

"Sue-ellen," Daddy said to Ma. "You done lost weight, eh, girl?"

"Stress" was all Ma said. Daddy nodded gloomily.

In the living room Daddy made a big fuss over my castle. He said he'd never seen nothing like it. Ma grunted.

"Sir Wallace, you have impressed me, sir," he said.

"It's brilliant," Heike agreed.

Daddy and her carefully stepped over one of my small towers and slid down onto our living room couch. Ma served Daddy a fat plate of pastelles, despite him and Heike saying they wouldn't consume any "junk." Pastelles were Daddy's favorite.

While he gobbled, Heike gawked at Daddy like he was somebody she didn't recognize. Between bites Daddy handed Ma a fat envelope and wished her a merry Christmas.

He opened my Christmas gift to him and loved it. I had bought him two bottles of cologne: buy one, get one free!

Then Heike started peeking around the living room.

My mother and her friend Mr. Jonathan never had nothing positive to say about any of Benny Rachpaul's latest sweethearts. He did have a lot of them. Maybe too many different ones.

"Are those Pez candy?" Heike asked. She had this funny accent. Ma nodded. Heike laughed. "Have you eaten all of these candies on the wall, Sue-ellen?"

Daddy's head was buried in pastelles.

"Actually," Ma said, "I just collect the dispensers."

Heike nodded. "They're beautiful. You have the atman of a child."

"Uh-huh," Ma grunted. "So you and Benjamin met at work?"

"Yes!" Heike said. "Yes, yes, yes, yes, yes." She squeezed his knee.

"Not my construction job," Daddy added. "We met at a party. Out in Jersey. She and I was both hired to entertain."

Uh, I should'a said—my father was a clown.

No, he actually was a *real* clown. At least, on weekends.

His main job was construction work. He installed toilets and hand dryers in buildings all around the city even though he had lived in this country illegal for years.

My father was born in Trinidad. A while back, though, he started working part-time as a clown for children's birthday parties.

He went by the name Rocky the Clown.

Last year I rode with him in his old dinged-up van to a kid's birthday party *waaaay* out in Long Island. I remember standing there in that family's gigantic backyard with their grass more green than any color green I had seen before and watching Rocky the Clown run and chase and laugh with them kids.

He hadn't been any kind of clown toward me and my brother. I always remember him being real quiet and kind of irritated.

Not fun.

This Heike lady was a professional fire-breather, Daddy told us. She would go to parties and shoot flames out of her mouth to entertain everybody. Sitting next to her on our couch, I studied her lips, searching for burns.

"Lolly, you want some?" Ma asked. "I'm 'bout to put this rice and peas back in the Frigidaire."

"Sue, will you stop calling the boy that?" Daddy complained. "We gave him Wallace as a name. That's a solid man's style. This 'Lolly' sounds like you're talking to your daughter."

"I think 'Lolly' is delightful," said Heike.

"Quit trying to make him into a female," Daddy told Ma.

Heike smiled at me with these big light-blue eyes and I suddenly wanted to smack her upside her head. Instead, I made my own eyes all wide and pointed toward the floor near her foot.

"Mouse," I whispered.

It took her a minute to understand, but when she got it, man, she screamed and flew into Daddy's arms. The only thing was, he was still sucking down his pastelles, which wound up all over his lap.

Ma was hot and made me clean the couch. When Rocky the Clown found out what I had told Heike, he glared at me.

"But I did see a mouse, Daddy," I said.

I didn't tell him the mouse had come with my new tablet. Afterward, I felt a little funny. I had been doing more and more stuff like this—mean stuff.

It was getting easier and easier.

8

Blam!

Us after-schoolers all jerked our heads toward the open door of our study room. We were sitting here, noses in our books, when we heard the sound of a gunshot. But there had been no gun shot.

The blast had been Big Rose.

She had forced the door to the room open by ramming her big butt into it. The slamming door had gone *blam!* and now we were all watching Big Rose's wide shoulders as she stepped in backward to the community center's study room.

"Dang, Big Rose!" Sunnshyne shouted. "You scared the crap out of me, girl!"

"Sunny, be quiet, please," Ms. Jenna said. "Rosamund, find a seat. *Quietly.*"

When Big Rose—aka Rosamund Major—just stood there in the door of the study room, with her huge back to us all, not saying nothing, Ms. Jen sighed and got up to see what was going on.

It was a mouse outside in the hall.

A real one.

Big Rose was standing in the doorway, fascinated by that mouse. Ms. Jen shooed it away and tried to pat Big Rose's shoulder, but that girl ducked away from her.

We all laughed.

Big Rose spun around and eyed all of us like she was surprised to see us sitting here. She just started coming to after-school in November. This girl had lived in St. Nick for a while, I think, and she'd been thrown out of too many after-schools to count.

Big Bad Rose liked to bang up other kids, we had heard.

And she was special too.

Big Rose stood there, surveying us all for a minute, then stomped to the chair that she usually sat in, all by itself, way on the other side of the room. I watched her and I traded grins with Sunnshyne and Vega.

Rosamund Major was the biggest and tallest kid in after-school. Maybe even the biggest and tallest kid in all of Harlem!

This girl had a watermelon head and this way of walking—or *stomping*—that looked like she was skipping rope on the moon; she kind of hopped into the air with every step she took. Her big ol' eyes flashed straight ahead, and her upper lip was always tucked inside her bottom one.

She fell into her chair and plunged into one of the tiny

books she always kept in her backpack. She would stay reading like that for most of after-school.

None of the other kids would say much, if anything, to her.

Ms. Jen would check in on her a couple of times.

Otherwise, it was like Big Rose wasn't even in our room. Except you couldn't help but watch her. Her head was like a dark planet that drew your eyes. I had never heard her speak.

I wasn't sure she knew how.

A little after we had had our snack, the community center got froze out. This happened sometimes. A freeze-out just meant that the staff closed and locked the doors to the building and nobody could come in or go out until the director said so.

Usually it was because there was some trouble in the neighborhood. Some type of danger like a beef between dealers or a gang battle.

This time, it was a shooting.

Some fourteen-year-old dude was shot in front of a bodega nearby. Sunny heard it was because the dude had slapped some girl the day before who was the girlfriend of some dealer.

Because of this, nobody could enter or leave the center until Mr. Ali said it was safe.

Vega was leaning in one corner of the room, laughing about something with Darrell B. But I sat at a table by myself.

On the floor somebody had tracked in some slush from outside. When I left our place this morning, it had been snowing. Now, this evening, it had all turned from bright white flakes to grubby gray mush.

This winter the snowstorms and darkness had really got to me. I wondered if I ever would be happy again.

The only thing that seemed to help was building my castle. When I was building, I forgot about everything else. But Ma was going to make me rip down the House of Moneekrom tonight, I knew it. And I didn't know what I was going to do then.

Really did not know.

Like I was losing control.

"Why did you used to be angry at your father?" I asked.

"I told you," Mr. Ali said. His voice got soft and lost inside his tiny office.

"No, you didn't!"

"I think I did tell you," Ali said. "And there's no need to shout."

"Look—" I started.

"Mr. Rachpaul, you are a brainy young man, but there's

some things you're keeping to yourself. Which is very dumb. I want to help."

I thought again about Jermaine and what had gone down between me and him before he passed. I guess it had been bothering me. It had been a bad way to end things with my brother.

"You tell me why you're so angry now and I'll tell you why I was so angry then." He raised a crooked eyebrow. "Deal?"

I sucked my teeth. "I don't got time for this. . . ."

"How's your father?" he asked.

"Aw, God! Why you bringing him up? He's okay," I said. "I guess."

"It's gotta be rough on him, losing a son. Parents aren't meant to bury their children. Kids, we basically grow up knowing that one day our parents are gonna leave us. But parents aren't conditioned to see their kids go on before them."

I had never really thought about that.

Mr. Ali leaned in closer across his desk. "Wallace, this might be a good time to get to know your father a little better, you know. You don't see him as much as you'd like."

"Well, that's on him, not me," I said. Ali saying this made me angry. "He's the father. He's supposed to make time to see me!"

"I understand, man. Calm down, brother."

I sat back in my seat and tried to look relaxed.

"Remember," Ali said, "your dad is having just as difficult a time adjusting to Jermaine's death as you are—mayhaps more. Consider that when you manage him. This could be a new, fortuitous opportunity for you and for your father to shape something better, adjust to a world without Jermaine."

I frowned.

"Be open," he said.

I'd rather keep closed. Nobody got me. Nobody cared.

I felt sick and hot.

9

My head was freezing.

A big wind whooshed down 125th Street. Made my head feel even frostier. I decided to speed up. My eyes were darting all around me, prepared to be ambushed.

Ever since Christmas Eve, I had felt like people were on the lookout for me.

I had only come out tonight because I was feeling really restless. Like I just had to get up and get out and move!

Even if I did get pounced on tonight, I still needed to walk.

I knew nobody else cared. And I was starting not to care too. I had hoped the weather out here would cool me down.

I stopped at Tuma's tiny shop on 125th. Tuma was my African hookup. His shop sold all kinds of stuff, from hair-care products to body oils to bootleg clothes to African statues.

Every time I asked the old dude what was his home

country, he dodged around. Like he was hiding the truth. Tuma had kids back in Africa, and he probably saw them more than my own father saw me. My brother had been more of a father to me than Benny Rachpaul.

I had felt safe around Jermaine. Just walking down the block with him, I knew couldn't nobody touch me. If Jermaine had still been alive, I wouldn't have felt so nervous stepping down 1-2-5, like I had been feeling.

No way.

Tuma's little shop didn't have no door. You just slid in off the street, and all the items he sold were sitting right there, out in the open. No AC in the summer. No real heat in the winter.

I couldn't sit out here in the cold all day like he did.

I stood there on the icy sidewalk waiting for Tuma to finish selling some hats to these white people. There were lots of white people that lived in Harlem. But at the same time, it was like they didn't really live here.

They had their own special places in Harlem that they went to that not many Black folks went to. At least none of the Black folks I knew. I mean, you never even saw them at any of our barbershops.

Not really.

I mean, if these white people lived in Harlem, why didn't they get their hair cut at our barbershops?

Maybe they thought Black barbers wouldn't know how to cut white heads. Or maybe the white people thought we wouldn't like them in there.

It was weird. I guess they liked staying invisible. And they liked to hide. Like Tuma. And Daddy.

Tuma sold this grinning couple two African hats for thirty bucks apiece. I knew I wasn't paying that!

"Lolly!" Tuma said. "Come inside, closer to the heat! How have you been, my boy? You remind me so much of my own son back home. How are you?"

He patted me on my back and pulled me near the space heater he had sitting there.

"Fiiine," I kinda sang like a kid. I didn't know why I did that. Sometimes I forgot how old I really was. "I need a hat, Tuma. A black-and-white African hat like the one you sold them."

Tuma scratched his beard and pulled the old quilt he had wrapped around him tighter. "I think I can help you. Yes, yes. I hope I still have one here for you."

He started searching through his bins. I turned around and peeked out at the sidewalk. I didn't see nobody lurking. I stepped closer to his electric heater to warm up my toes.

"Here you are, Lolly!" Tuma said. "My last!" He handed me one of the knit hats that was shaped like a big hockey puck. It had tassels coming out the top.

"This one's white and *blue*," I said. "How much?"

"For you—ten dollars."

I bulged my eyeballs.

"Okay, okay," he said. "Since you are my old friend— I will give it to you for seven."

I threw back my head and stared at him. We stood like that for a while. Then I acted like I had to go and handed his hat back to him. I started to step off. He sold me the hat for three dollars.

I snapped it on my head right then.

As I left, I saw Tuma unpack a whole nother box of them same hats and stack them on a shelf in his shop.

The wind was *really* whipping around here, fourteen stories up. I was glad I'd bought this hat. In the dark, I tore another sheet of paper out of my notebook and started to fold again.

The door to get up here was broke and so was the door alarm. You just needed to jiggle the lock to get it open.

I stopped to look out over St. Nick Houses, all lit up in the night. Being up here made me feel better. From where I now sat, on the roof of my own building, you could gaze out across all of Central Harlem.

At night like this, Harlem was a big glowing crossword puzzle. You could see how the streetlights lined the avenues, crisscrossing each other. It was all a big grid.

To my left, the glowing grid got all dark. St. Nicholas Park. It was mostly trees and hardly any lampposts.

I leaned over the edge of my building's roof and peeked down. Some girl was walking along one of the footpaths. She was nervous, the way her head kept darting around her. Probably coming home from work.

I tossed my plane out. The wind caught it and jerked it downward. My plane whirled around a bit before getting sucked between the buildings.

It was too windy tonight to fly my paper planes, really.

They were all just getting crumpled up.

Destruction.

I peeked down again at the footpaths fourteen stories below. That girl had disappeared. The wind blew up again and the chills itched straight down my back.

It was a long way down to the ground from up here. A few times, people who lived at St. Nick had jumped. Couldn't take the lives they were living, I guess.

If Jermaine was here, I wouldn't be scared of nothing. He was my protector. It hurt, thinking back on how he had stopped talking to me before Halloween.

I wished I hadn't done what I did.

Tonight I was so high up. A big blast could take me right over this edge. I wondered what it would feel like to fall.

Bad thoughts.

Bad memories.

10

"Flip it *gentle*, Lolly," Jermaine said. "Look, it's breaking up."

My brother stood tall behind me. He stepped forward and grabbed my wrist. My hand was still holding real tight on to the plastic spatula. Moving my own hand with his, we lifted the pancake together. It flipped over gently onto the dark, hot skillet.

Grease popped like firecrackers.

I jumped backward, bumping into Jermaine and landing on his sneakers.

Then *he* flipped like a pancake.

"Why you gotta step all over my clean new sneaks with your grimy house slippers!" Jermaine yelled at me, pushing me off his shoes.

I tried to shove him, but his hand palmed my forehead, keeping me away. Laughing, I kept snatching at Jermaine. He grinned at me, teasing, holding on to my head.

"Yo, Loll!" Jermaine said. "Loll! Stop playing. You play too much."

"*You* play too much!" I said. I had been breathing hard, straining, trying to get at him. I stopped trying and stood there in our apartment's kitchen, glaring at him, crossing my arms over my chest.

Jermaine stared back at me, shook his head and laughed. "That's better. Oh snap! See what you did? Your pancake's burning!"

All this I'm talking about? It had happened a *looooong* time ago.

Like maybe three long years ago, when I was, like, nine years old and just a kid. Jermaine had just finished high school. At first, he had worked at that jacked-up grocery store on Frederick Douglass Boulevard and 127th, but he soon left that and started working at this barbershop that used to be on St. Nick Av'.

Rockit had told me that him and Jermaine had started there around the same time. Jermaine had really liked working at that barbershop. The first month they had him sweeping up all the cut curls from off the floor. After he had done that awhile, he told me, they had started him doing other stuff that paid more.

He had liked making that money.

Jermaine examined the brown pancake and said, "It

ain't too bad," relieved. "Now we put this one on the plate. And start over. Pour a little batter into the middle of the skillet. Wait. Watch it. That's good. And when you start to see them bubbles bubble up in the middle of the pancake, then you know it's good to go: you can flip it then. But gentle, Loll. *Gentle.*"

Jermaine plopped down at the kitchen table and started reading his newspaper. The business section. He would always bring it home with him from the barbershop, where they got the paper delivered every day.

I stood in front of our stove and watched the pancake cook in the pan.

"It's nice having light again, right?" Jermaine said, eyes on his paper. "You can't read at night in the dark." He shook his head.

We both glanced at the bright lamp he had just plugged into the end of a big, thick orange extension cord. The cord snaked in through our window, which was cracked just enough to let it pass under.

Jermaine had got tired of trying to read his papers by candlelight for the past week after all the power in our apartment went out.

Back then was when Daddy had lived with us too. Before him and Ma broke up. Daddy used to have a hard time working steady, so that meant that my parents' cash was never steady.

But that wasn't why our lights was shut off.

In public housing, electricity was included in your rent. They would evict you onto the streets first before they'd ever switch off your power.

The reason why we didn't have no juice—along with half of our floor—was because of a short circuit in the walls.

Blowout.

We had waited a whole week for the managers to fix the electricity, but they still hadn't. Like I said, the city didn't fix nothing!

Jermaine solved the problem by asking our next-door neighbor Mrs. Jenkins to let us pass that big, thick orange electric cord between our apartments. Her half of the floor still had power. That electric cord looped out our window, seven stories above the sidewalks, and right into the window of the Jenkinses' apartment next door. Jermaine had handed her some money to smooth things over, so everybody was happy.

I remember wondering what was gonna happen when my father and mother found out that night.

"What in the devil?" Daddy Rachpaul said later when he walked into the kitchen. He had spent the whole day hanging around construction sites in the city, looking for work. That whole week, we had all got used to coming home to darkness and candlelight.

So when Daddy walked in and saw me and Jermaine

frying pancakes next to a lightbulb lit up, he was surprised.

And happy.

"My little Fox!" Daddy said to Jermaine. Daddy laughed and cupped the top of Jermaine's head. "We have at least one other genius in the house, eh? But what'll we do if the janitor sees?" Daddy peeked out the window. "Tomorrow the management'll spot that orange cord hanging about and they might say it's not safe."

"Well, I figure we only need lights at night," Jermaine said, still reading. He glanced up from his paper. "When the sun comes up, we haul in the extension cord until the next night. The building won't see nothing."

"You *are* a sly genius," Daddy said. "Come here, boy!" He grabbed Jermaine up from his chair and pinned him against the refrigerator. Jermaine's newspaper pages floated down to the linoleum.

"Hey!" Jermaine yelled. "Daddy! Ow!"

Daddy Rachpaul grinned at him and told him to fight back. Jermaine just kept yelling at him. Daddy was holding him up by his arm, Jermaine's back against the fridge, my brother's feet on tippy-toes.

"My arm! My arm!" Jermaine kept yelling.

I watched them with one eye, but kept my second eye on my third pancake like Jermaine had told me. It had started to bubble at the center, which was interesting. My brother getting jacked against the fridge like that happened all the time.

It was boring.

I flipped my pancake.

"You can be a sly fox in the head," Daddy told Jermaine, "but you can man up too. You not gonna man up and free yourself from me?"

Jermaine finally whacked Daddy's chest and that made Daddy feel better, so he let him slide down off the fridge. Jermaine bent over and rubbed his arm.

Daddy turned to look at the electrical cord again. "I guess I'm gonna have to break off some cheddar for that Mrs. Jenkins next door." He rubbed his smooth chin. "I wonder how much cash that nosy bat'll want for all this messy-mess?"

"I took care of it."

Daddy turned to Jermaine, who was still massaging his sore arm. "What?" Daddy asked him, surprised. "You paid her? How much? With what?"

Jermaine stood up straight. "Not much," he said. "I got us some groceries too: bread, soda, lots of canned stuff. Lolly wanted pancakes."

Daddy stared at Jermaine for a minute and was about to open his mouth again when we all turned our heads toward the sound of the front door. It was Ma coming home.

Ma looked exhausted, and didn't seem to like the electrical-cord arrangement that Jermaine had set up. But she was happy too.

She had just got hired at a new job doing store security downtown. Daddy Rachpaul got so happy after hearing that. Though Ma tried to dodge him, he kissed her and dragged her away, back into their room, and shut the door.

Jermaine and me went back to our pancake-flipping.

A new job meant money for stuff.

I thought about my brother giving that money to Mrs. Jenkins next door and him buying groceries and I wished I had a job to help out around the house. I remember asking Jermaine if I could start sweeping floors at the barbershop after school.

It didn't seem like that hard of a thing to do. I was only nine, but how old did you have to be to sweep up old hair?

When I asked him if I could work at the barbershop, Jermaine, who had just finished flipping a pancake, flung on me all of a sudden. He whipped the spatula in front of my face and little bits of hot oil flicked at me, burning my eyeball.

I cried out.

He carried me over to the sink and washed the oil out of my eye.

My eyes still shut, I heard Ma yell out from the bedroom, "What's going on out there? Lolly? You okay?"

"Open your eye," I heard Jermaine say. "Open your eye, Lolly."

I opened both of them slowly. All I could see were my brother's big brown eyes staring right into mine, a few inches away. He was frowning.

"Can you see?" he asked me.

I nodded.

He sucked his teeth as loud as Ma did. "You okay," he said then, yelling, "We okay, Ma!"

Ma: "What happened!"

Jermaine grabbed his jacket off the back of the kitchen chair. "Nothing! It ain't nothing! We okay!"

"You boys play too much!" Daddy yelled back.

Jermaine turned to me and this time stuck his finger in my face. I shrank.

"I don't want you coming around the barbershop," he told me. He waited a minute and seemed to be thinking about something. "I see your skinny little butt around here too much as it is." He snapped on his jacket. "I get sick of seeing you every day, man. We sleep in the same tiny room, eat in the same tiny kitchen, same tiny apartment. . . . I get tired of having you all up on me, all the time, Lolly."

My eyes got wet.

"I don't want you around," Jermaine said. "Especially not down at the barbershop. Promise me you won't go down

73

there. No matter who tries to send you down there, promise me you won't do it."

A tear fell down my cheek, but I didn't say nothing. Angry, Jermaine lurched toward me.

"I promise," I said quick. "I won't go to the barbershop. I'll stay away from you."

My brother looked at me then real sad, but with a weird half smile. He started to reach out to me, but stopped when he saw me move away.

"I'm going out," he said, and was gone.

I remember crying and running to our bedroom and spending the next hour building a pirate Lego set. After that, I felt better.

That was probably the first time I remember getting relief from diving into my Lego world.

They sucked me into another place when my real place was too much. And now it wasn't just getting taken to a new place. It was about going to an old place too, someplace familiar that I'd been to before.

My daddy maybe was in that place.

And Jermaine maybe.

Mr. Ali thought me getting to know my father better would help with whatever I'd been feeling lately. But in the back of my head, I didn't really know how much Daddy wanted me around.

11

"**M**y cousin Frito was the kid that got capped in front of that bodega yesterday," Vega whispered over my ear. I just stared at him. "He's okay, though," he said. "Mami found out they tagged him in the shoulder. She's coming to get me now. Don't want me going back home alone."

Vega eased down beside me. His seat creaked. We both glanced toward Ms. Jen. I didn't know why. I guess to see if she was watching. She was lost in her earphones.

I whispered at Vega, "Frito was the one that slapped Shark James's fiancée?"

He nodded.

"*Stupid,*" I whispered.

I hadn't never met the street gangsta known around here as Shark James, but I had heard enough grubbiness about him to know that you don't be going around slapping his baby ma.

"*Look,*" Vega said, showing me the screen on his phone.

He was holding it low, underneath the table, so Ms. Jenna couldn't see.

"What?" I said, squinting at his screen.

"I got this message from Frito yesterday before he got shot. Them two boys that was following us, Harp and Gully, they told Frito again yesterday that they want him to join they crew."

His finger dragged over his screen so I could read the message. I just shook my head after reading it. Harp and Gully had been recruiting *hard* for their crew. I took out my phone and Vega and me scrolled through some of the threads online.

All these different crews had been posting threats toward one another. Telling each other that their crew was the best and that they were going to stomp out the rest. I didn't understand why they posted all this online, where anybody could read it. Harp and Gully's crew had even made a stupid music video, rapping about how they were going to shoot up folks they had beef with.

Right when I was about to show Vega the video, I suddenly flew backward in my chair. At first, I thought I was going to fall flat on my back, but then I stopped and somehow jerked up into the air, right out of my seat. I spun around in the air and dangled upside down.

Somebody grabbed my phone out of my hands. I screamed. I couldn't help it.

"Mr. Rachpaul!" I heard Mr. Ali shout out. "Is your homework stored on your phone?"

Still upside down, dangling from one of Mr. Ali's arms, all I could do was yell. I could see everybody else in the room running toward me. I couldn't see Ali's face.

"That doesn't sound like the answer of an intelligent young man," Ali said. "Methinks you and I shall have another chat." While Sunny, Daryl and even Vega laughed, Mr. Ali carried me upside down out of the room, down the hall and into a dark space.

I didn't know where I was. I was getting woozy from hanging this way.

"Mr. Ali!" I yelled. "I'm sorry! Put me down! I'm dizzy!"

The lights flickered on. I could tell we were in the storage room. He let my head touch the floor, then folded the rest of my body on top of me until I was crumpled up on the tiles.

I laughed. "Hey, man!" I shouted. "This floor is *unclean*, man!"

"You calling me 'man' again, Wallace? I am not one of your playmates."

"Are you cracking up?" I tried to act gangsta, but I was grinning and laughing too hard.

Ali watched me with his slanted face, like he was about to bust out laughing himself. He yelled, "Next time I catch you celebrating 'hood fame' and grimy gang threats in *my* after-school, I'm going to snatch that shiny phone your mama gave you and lock you up in this storage room here!"

I sucked my teeth at him. My teeth smacks was almost as loud as Ma's.

"Lock you in here with all the cockroaches and cat-rats," he went on.

I sat there in the dust on the floor and snorted again. "I wish you would!" I shouted at him. "If you did that, my moms would knock you— *Hey!*"

Mr. Ali had started to close the door. Behind him in the hall I could see Vega and the others gawking at me with smiles on their faces. I hopped up and tried to grab the door handle before he could shut it.

Ka-klick!

Too late.

I was locked inside the gigantic storage room by myself. I punched at the closed door and laughed some more. Ali was crazy-mazey!

"Oh, so this is *fun?*" I heard Ali say, muffled from the other side. "We shall all see how fun it is when those cat-rats creep out and start chasing you!" The others laughed at this.

"Don't worry, Loll!" Vega shouted. "When the cat-rats come, just jog in circles!" More chuckles. "There's enough space in there to play dodgeball!"

I folded my arms and stepped backward, away from the

door. I listened to them all giggle at Vega's cracks. But then something began to jiggle loose in my brain.

Was it from being held upside down too long?

Arms still folded, I gradually turned around and studied the large room I was standing in.

There was a lot of space here. The ceiling must'a been at least twenty feet high. The only furniture was a bunch of folding metal chairs and wooden ladders leaned up against the walls.

A loud sound began to rumble. I glanced up at the big heating vent on the wall. Warm air had started shooting out of it. It felt good, blowing on my face.

That thing in my brain started to jiggle loose a little bit more.

By the time Mr. Ali had opened the door and ordered me to come out, I was so deep-thinking that I barely noticed him standing behind me, speaking at the back of my head.

I was somewhere else, another world.

And I loved it.

12

Goofy Valentine's.

And goofy Sunny was handing out chocolate-covered pecans to everybody at after-school.

Quintesha.

Daryl R.

Darrell B.

Me, she gave a whole bag.

Of course she gave a few to her "best girl" April Etokakpan. And Sunny even gave one to Vega, her arch-enemy. She gave one to Mr. Ali and the two other teachers on staff.

Like I said, she gave one to everybody in after-school.

Except Big Rose.

I didn't care that Sunny had left Big Rose out. Well, I guess I did care, but in the wrong way. Somewhere deep inside of me, somewhere buried in my chest, it felt good to see Rosamund get left out.

If I wasn't happy, then why should anybody else be?

I swallowed one of the candies. The chocolate was dark and bitter.

Sunny had said that her and her new *boyfriend* had made them by hand the day before. When Sunny said "boyfriend," she gazed straight ahead. Her friend April E. glanced at her, then at me, then back at her. They both giggled.

Girls were weird.

I slung another chocolate pecan into my mouth and watched Big Rose sit by herself in the opposite corner of our study room. That Big Rose was a weird girl too, I thought.

Sunny said she had heard Big Rose was homeschooled by her grandmother and only came here for after-school. I let the last of my candy slide down my throat and thought about just how weird Big Rose was. She never once glanced up toward the rest of us when Sunnshyne was dancing around, handing out her candy.

Rose was in her own world.

Far away.

Outer solar system, man.

"These candies is delicious," Quintesha said to Sunny. "You and your man need to make more. Just for me."

April E. nodded. "My girl Sunny can cook!" she said.

"Oh, girl, that's easy," said Sunny. "One of my many talents."

Vega rolled his eyes. "*Average* chocolate, Sunny," he said.

"I tasted better candy I found in our sofa." He grinned and sat down next to me and started to unpack his violin from its case.

"You know something, *Casimiro*?" Sunny said to Vega. "You are really an offensive little boy. I just wanted to wish everybody a happy Valentine's." She glanced across the room at Big Rose, who was still so into whatever the hell it was that she was reading.

Vega sat his violin across his lap. He had named it 'Ye. He watched Sunny and ran his fingers over 'Ye's strings.

Sunny opened her mouth again. "My best girl April E. and me have started a business."

Everybody got quiet. Vega plucked a string on his violin. It sounded like a noise made by a cartoon character who was a idiot. Me and Quintesha snorted. Sunny didn't approve.

"Huh?" Daryl R. said to Sunny. "Business? We gotta pay for these chocolates? You said they was free."

"No, dummy! Not this. We are detectives," April E. announced.

"EDK Investigators," said Sunny. "We printed the name of our new business on the candy wrappers. See?"

"It was her *boyfriend's* idea," April said, and locked eyes with Sunnshyne.

Honestly, April E. was a pretty girl. And actually cool

when she wasn't around Sunny, getting contaminated by her best friend's glow of evil.

And Sunny didn't have no boyfriend. She was too young. I knew her moms wouldn't allow that.

I unfolded my candy wrapper that I had crumpled up and flung on the table. Someone had written in neat letters: EDK INVESTIGATORS.

"You stupid," Quintesha, laughing, told these two girls.

"You think you detectives now?" Vega asked them, like he couldn't believe it. Daryl started to snicker too. This pissed Sunny off.

"Our *first* major mystery to solve," she said all loud, like saying it loud made it sound more real, "is what Lolly's been doing in that storage room all week."

April smiled at me like only her smile could get me to confess.

These St. Nick girls...

"Ohhhhh," Darrell said, leaning over Daryl's shoulder. Darrell squinted closer at what Daryl was doodling on his new tablet. "Are those crew tags?" he asked.

"Yep," Daryl said. "I'm sketching up one for Mile High Money."

Darrell scrunched his round face at him. "You MHM?"

Daryl shook his head. "My boy one. I'm doing they crew a favor, coming up with this new logo for them."

"You shouldn't be messing around with them gangs, Daryl," Quintesha said. "They get boys *big* into trouble. You know?"

Daryl R. shrugged and kept drawing on his tablet with his index finger. His crew design was a fist and another hand holding up two fingers, with a Glock and a dove in the background.

The other kids liked it, so he started showing them more screens of his other stuff, along with some really dope drawings his cousin in Missouri had emailed him.

It got me thinking that I should do more with the tablet Benny Rachpaul got me for Late Christmas. Maybe I could make some designs like Daryl's.

"Here's another one of my cousin Jayden's grafs," he said, showing us the graffiti scribbles.

Sunnshyne scrunched her face at it. "It's okay, but what's with all them loop-de-loops in his drawings?"

"That's his sign," Daryl told us. "And it ain't a loop-de-loop. It's a infinity symbol. It means 'forever.'"

"Nobody lives forever," Sunny said real swift, and we dove back into our homework.

But Vega began to play this thing called Cello Suite no. 1, by that old musician Bach. That's all he'd been playing on his violin for the past couple of months.

The song was pretty, but I was nauseous from hearing it over and over.

Sunny must'a been having trouble concentrating too, because she glanced up from her book and across the area at Big Rose. Frankenstein Girl was still reading her book when Sunny plopped a chocolate-covered candy down on the table in front of her.

As soon as Sunny had sat back down across from me at the table, we both watched Big Rose unwrap the candy and fling it in her mouth. I was surprised at Sunny for being nice like that, finally giving her a candy.

Was it Valentine's Day that had made Sunnshyne do it?

The evil way I was feeling, I'd'a preferred if she *hadn't* given one to Big Rose.

Just then, Big Rose hopped up from her seat and started moaning. She ran by our table with tears in her eyes, using her fingers to grab at and scrub her tongue.

She wasn't skipping this time, but running straight as a bullet.

We all watched her sprint out into the hallway toward the water fountain. All except Sunny, whose eyes stayed stuck to her math book.

"Our chocolates come pecan-flavored," she whispered without looking up, "and jalapeño-flavored."

We all croaked.

Sunny drilled deeper into her math book and smirked.

· ✛ ✛ ·

Toting my orange backpack over one shoulder, I crept down the hall in the community center. I hated to do this—interrupt Mr. Ali's Sunnshyne roast—but I had wrapped up my homework half an hour ago and I was ready to get busy.

"Well, me and Ray made all different types of flavors," I could hear Sunny say. "I guess one of the hot ones got mixed in with the sweet by accident."

Mr. Ali had been hollering at her. She wore a fake-sad face. Suddenly Mr. Ali whipped around toward me.

"Wallace?" he said. "What you doing out here? Did you know about this chocolate-covered jalapeño?"

I shook my head. "Not until it was all over," I said.

"Good," he said, spinning back on Sunny.

"Mr. Ali?" I said.

"Get back in there and finish your homework," he snapped at me. Then, before I could say anything: "While I conversate with Ms. Dixon-Knight here."

"I did!" I said.

"What?"

"I did my homework, Mr. Ali. *Early.* I want you to let me in. It's time for me to go inside the storage room."

Sunnshyne squinted her eyes at me when she heard me say this.

"*Oh,*" said Mr. Ali. "That's right. Tell Lady Bug to let you in. Tell her I said it's okay. Now, Ms. Sunnshyne, did you stop to think what could've happened if Big Rose had been allergic to jalapeños? We could've had to rush her to the ER."

I rushed off to get Ms. Jen, hoping she wouldn't give me no problems. For real, if I had to wait any longer, I'd die.

It was that serious.

13

"**M**y *bibi* told me that if you do it with a girl before you're old enough, your *thing* will shrivel away like a twig in a fire."

We all paused a minute to recognize what Mohammed had just said, then we busted up laughing. All five of us.

Except for Mohammed.

It felt good to laugh.

At night me and some of my friends sat on the cold stone steps, deep inside St. Nicholas Park. It was pretty big, but not as big as Central Park. St. Nicholas Park was more long than wide, and a big hill.

Tons of trees sloped all around us. Stairs rose up the hill to where Hamilton Heights and City College were. We had to look out for police because the park had shut for the night, and we also had a lit loosey.

None of us was older than fourteen.

"Yo, Mohammed," Daryl Reynolds said, giggling. "Your grandma told you that for reals?"

Mohammed nodded. You could tell he didn't understand why we had all laughed at him. Kofi took a drag from the cigarette they was passing around and tried to share it with Mohammed, who waved it away, pouting.

"Mo, what made you believe that?" Kofi asked him.

Mohammed didn't answer. He crunched one of the French fries he gripped in a greasy bag on his lap.

"You dumbass African," Cyril said in the dark.

"Hey! Cyril, don't crack on Africans," Kofi said. "I am African and I wouldn't believe what Mohammed's *bibi* told him. Besides, you *coconuts* are far more dumb than us Africans."

"Oh snap," Freddy said, trying to instigate a throwdown.

"Lolly, man, you gonna let him get away with calling you and Cyril coconuts?" Daryl R. asked me, laughing. "You two are the only West Indians sitting on these steps."

Every now and then I had heard the term "coconut." It was how some people dogged out families from the Caribbean. The word usually made me mad, but I knew that Kofi was only acting up.

Kofi sucked his teeth and grabbed my shoulder. "I wasn't talking about Lolly," he said. "He and his mother have had a rough time. Lolly is the *good* sort of coconut." We all laughed. "Not like my man Cyril up there."

Cyril tossed an empty bag onto Kofi's head. Kofi threw it back at him.

"Yo, Mo!" Freddy yelled. "Pass me some French fries!"

"Yo, Loll," Daryl said to me. "April E. got a fat booty, don't she?"

I nodded, grinning.

"Not as big as Tisha's!" Freddy called out, munching on fries.

"Shut up, Freddy!" Daryl said. "But April talk too much." He took a drag on the cigarette and passed it around. "All them girls talk too much," Daryl complained.

"I heard her and Sunny are acting like detectives now!" Freddy called down. Daryl blew out air, disgusted. "My man Butteray Jones caught them snooping," Freddy said.

"Butteray Jones?" Daryl asked.

"Butteray Jones!" Freddy shouted.

"Man, what kind of name is that?" Cyril asked.

"He from down South. They named him that because when he was a baby, he used to eat sticks'a butter rolled in sugar," Freddy said.

"Eww!" Cyril said.

"They nasty down South," said Daryl.

"His parents own that new restaurant on Sugar Hill," Freddy went on. "Anyway, Butteray Jones caught Sunny and her girl investigating around here. Up in this park. Like they was police or something searching for somebody."

"I wouldn't mind being a cop," Cyril added.

Daryl raised a eyebrow. "You *would*, Cyril."

Kofi laughed and said, "I'm gonna code." He handed me the loosey. "What about you, Loll?" Kofi asked. "What you wanna be?"

Holding our cigarette in my hand, I thought on this question for a long while. "I don't know," I said. I shrugged. "I don't really know, Kof."

I had never smoked before, but took a quick puff on the cigarette and tried to pass it away.

"That's not how you do it!" Daryl said. "You gotta inhale!"

They were all watching.

I tried again, inhaling deep. The smoke flew down my throat and a bunch of coughing came back up. I was hacking so hard, I felt like I was about to throw up. Daryl and Kofi patted my back.

Smoking cigarettes was like sucking on the exhaust pipe of a car with a running motor. I could hear everybody laughing. I felt so queasy.

Why did people smoke, anyhow?

I leaned over the steps and stuck my head between my legs. I finished coughing and spat out something.

"Oh my goodness," I heard Freddy say.

"Jesus," I heard Cyril say.

"Ohhhh," I heard Daryl say.

I lifted my head to see what was going on. I hoped it wasn't no cop, out patrolling the park. That was the last thing I needed now.

But I was staring at a pair of glowing yellow eyes, floating in the dark. They were hovering about fifteen feet away, down the steps from us. We all sat still as statues as the shining eyes slowly came closer, up the hill.

We heard a *click-clack* on the stone steps.

The eyes were attached to what looked like a dog. But no way was this a dog. This thing was more like a *wolf.*

It stood about three feet high and was gray with a white belly and long tail. The hair was pretty lengthy and silky. On top of its head were these two pointy ears. Its nose and legs were black and way longer than any dog's.

It had long claws on its feet too. They made that *click-clack* sound.

The wolf-thing came a few feet away from us and just stood there.

"What is it?" Cyril whispered.

It glared right at us. I hoped it wasn't going to eat us. If it had wanted to, we wouldn't have stood a chance. It licked its mouth. I could see its breath in the cold night air.

Mohammed tossed it a French fry.

"Don't feed it, Mohammed!" Daryl whispered. "Are you crazy?"

The wolf-thing snapped up the fry and tilted its head

at us like it wanted more. Mohammed launched his whole bag of French fries at it. While it was chomping on those, we slowly stood and tiptoed up the steps to the Hamilton Heights part of Harlem.

I felt safer, out of the dark trees in the park and back around streetlights with people strolling and car horns. We avoided the park and traveled down Amsterdam Av' to 125th Street, then cut back over toward Central Harlem.

We didn't want to take any chances of that wolf-thing hunting us.

At Morningside Avenue we saw these three beautiful women walking toward us. They were headed toward all the cafés and restaurants. All three of them were caramel-skinned and two of them was wearing white dress coats while the last one was wearing stripes. All six of us boys stopped at the corner to watch these ladies glide by.

They even smiled at us. "What's happening, young brothers," the prettiest one said.

"Hello," we all said.

They kept on. I think I heard the one in stripes call us cute.

After they had passed, Daryl tried to act like he was about to follow them and try to rap to them. Those women were maybe two times his age. And I think he was serious about it too, until Kofi told him to come on and stop acting stupid.

While we walked, I used the free Wi-Fi to do a search. It turned out, what we had seen in the park must'a been a wild coyote. I told the other guys and they couldn't believe it.

Over the past few years, the police had caught four coyotes in Harlem and delivered them to the Bronx Zoo. The article I read on my phone said the animals were coming down into Washington Heights and Harlem from Westchester, just north of New York City.

They were searching for food and a nice place to live since human beings had been taking over their territories and forests. Driving them out.

I guessed our coyote had picked St. Nicholas Park as his new home.

I wouldn't report that animal to the police. The article said they hadn't attacked nobody, but just wanted food. It also said that they were so scarce in the city, you shouldn't feel scared if you met one; you should feel lucky.

We did feel lucky to have met that thing. It made us feel excited and extra alive.

There had been something beautiful and scary about it.

That Harlem coyote deserved to be free, just like everybody else. At least, he could be happy in the park, I thought.

I just wouldn't be hanging out in St. Nick Park at night.

And I definitely wouldn't be smoking.

14

Ka-klick!

Over the past week, that noise had become my most favorite sound in the world. The *ka-klick* of the unlocking door to the big storage room in the community center.

Mr. Ali stepped to my side so I could go in. "There you go, Wallace," he said to me. I tried to move past him, but he blocked me with an arm. "You're never gonna tell me?"

"Tell you what?" I asked. He just stared at me. I sighed and rolled my eyes back in my head. "Jermaine stopped talking to me just before he died, okay? We had had a argument."

"Argument?"

"Okay, Mr. Ali? We used to argue all the time in that little room. Okay?"

He stood there quiet for a minute, still blocking my way. "That is progress," Ali finally said. "Talking about it will make you feel better. Always does."

"You talk to me about what your father did to your face," I told him, "and I'll tell you what me and Jermaine argued about."

Ali pulled his arm back so I could pass and pointed his thumb into the storage room. "Your world awaits!"

Just as I strolled inside, I heard the heater begin to rumble. Warm air started to flow out of the wall vent. He was right, this *was* my world, I thought.

One of the tricky things about castles was getting your turrets lined up. When I had been creating my first version of the House of Moneekrom up in our apartment, that building had seemed big, but it wasn't really.

Now with my new, expanded version of the House of Moneekrom, here in the storage room, it had become harder to know if my turrets facing each other were the same height. It was harder down here because the size of my castle had tripled.

I could no longer use only my eyes to guess heights and widths and all that. I had to count, measure, get more technical.

So far, none of the other after-schoolers knew what I had been up to in here. Nobody except Vega. Sunny acted like she was about to *'splode* if her "detective agency" didn't expose why I'd been coming into the storage room after homework.

Two days ago, when I let Vega in here for the first time, he couldn't believe what I had done.

"*Mira*, Lolly," Vega had said. "Your castle! It's huge!"

I showed him my castle walls and how I had constructed new merlons along them. Instead of using the tiny Lego bricks, I had started building with larger ones since I now had so much more space—an entire, huge storage room to build my fantasy fortress.

And Yvonne kept dropping off more and more trash bags filled with Legos for me, so who knew how *huge-mongous* I could go.

I was creating my own new world and getting lost in it.

Just being here with my Legos, building, I could almost feel my brother with me. Like he was actually in this room, watching over me. I could really feel someone.

Suddenly the heating vent across the room went quiet.

Standing there alone, I now heard another noise behind me, like somebody breathing heavy. Someone *was* standing there.

My neck got all prickly.

Jermaine? I wondered.

I swung around and peeped Big Rose's face in the doorway. Ms. Jen had forgot to lock the door this time. Big

Rose had opened it and stuck her big ugly head through the crack.

Big Rose stared at me, then at my castle, then back at me again.

I pointed at her to warn her back.

She frowned and gave me an evil look. I wondered if she blamed me for the jalapeño chocolate incident. This girl might'a thought me and Sunny had been in on it together.

I took a step toward Big Rose, but I heard Ms. Jen calling her. The girl disappeared back into the hall, *ka-klick*ing the door behind her. Alone in the dim, dusty room, I could still see her dumb round eyes, rubbernecking.

My world felt hijacked.

15

ing!

The doors opened to the elevator just outside our front door. I walked behind our next-door neighbor, old Mrs. Jenkins, and we both stepped between the elevator doors. Mr. Williams from the tenth floor was already in the elevator, and another boy my age I hadn't seen before. After the doors shut, Mrs. Jenkins turned to me again, her eyes shining.

"My Lord, Lolly," she said. "You sure are getting grown."

"Thank you, ma'am," I said, shifting my weight. The other kid didn't look at me.

Just then, my phone chirped. I knew it had to be Vega. He had been waiting on me downstairs for a minute.

"They finally got around to fixing this elevator," Mrs. Jenkins said to me. "How's Sue-ellen?"

"Fiiine," I kinda sang. "They got her working too hard down at the courts."

"Tell her I said she's blessed to have that job. Thank the Lord."

"Yes, ma'am."

I was glad that for the rest of the elevator ride, she didn't say nothing. Old folks are okay, but I never know what to speak to them. We flew straight from the seventh floor down to the first, with only the pissy elevator smell to focus on.

When the doors opened, Vega was waiting there. I could only see the back of his shiny black parka until he spun around, rolling his eyes.

"*Mira,* Lolly!" he said. "I been waiting on you forever!"

"You're dramatic," I said.

I watched the boy from the elevator step outside. Before he left, he had passed Vega a look like he had wanted to stick him. Vega just glared at him until he disappeared outside the doors of the lobby. Then Vega frowned at me.

"You got me waiting on you in my new coat," he said, complaining some more.

"Shut up, applehead. Let's go do this."

The D train rumbled along underground with me and Vega sitting inside. It wasn't crowded. We had one of its ugly plastic orange seats between us. Vega was thumbing through stuff on his phone.

I got bored. I pulled out my tablet from my parka and started doodling. I glanced at the subway map again. It was posted just above the pom-pom hat of this old dude, sitting beside me.

On the map I could see the number of stops we had to go before we would be getting off. I squinted at the tiny blue line on the map that was supposed to be the Harlem River.

My eyes raced over the ceiling of the subway car, and I imagined the icy river water that was running way up above us.

The Harlem River divided Manhattan from the Bronx. And the D train ran in a tunnel from Manhattan to the Bronx, but I had never really thought too much about all that river water above my head.

You didn't see the river, so you didn't think about it.

New York City was surrounded by water that nobody ever thought about. I lived on an island, really. An island inside an island inside an island.

Stranded.

I sighed and wondered how many people had died in these waters. Either by jumping into them themselves, or by somebody pushing them.

How many people had even died in New York City since it'd been around?

A lot of dead, buried bodies, man.

I started sketching a river with bodies beneath it on my tablet.

We rose up out the Fordham subway station in the Boogie Down Bronx. I didn't know why the old folks called it that, the Boogie Down.

What was a "boogie," anyhow? Was it like a booger?

That would be nauseating.

I hung the hood of my blue parka over my head and let the rest of my coat float behind me. It was cold today, but I was feeling hot inside.

It took me a minute to figure out which direction to head down Fordham Road, but Vega had found it already on his map. I scrunched up my face and we started walking. My stomach started to flutter a little, from me being so nervous, I guess.

This was a bad day.

A bad day to be in the Bronx.

Lately, my days were bad days to be anywhere. The badness usually started in the mornings right after I woke. Sometimes I would wake up carefree, and then it would hit me.

Jermaine.

And I would feel that heavy rock grow weightier on my chest, while I was lying there on my back, still in bed.

The rock would just sink dead into the center of my chest, right into my heart. Like it was sinking into mud.

"Yo, is Big Rose still eyeballing you in your storage room?" Vega asked.

"She tries to, but Lady Bug keeps calling her away."

"That is weird," he said. "That is a weird girl, *manin*."

Fordham Road was crazy crowded. This street had all kinds of stores and places to eat. It was like the 125th Street of the Bronx. I kept trying to pay attention to everybody around me, just in case some thug tried to start something.

This wasn't our hood.

"Yo, man," Vega said, "I hope that girl don't go bonkers on you up in the center, man."

"Bonkers?"

"*Bonkers!* Yeah. You know she ain't right." He tapped the side of his head. "She be spying on you *hard* every day you leave for the storage room to work on Harmonee. . . ."

I shrugged. Vega was getting dramatic again.

Harmonee was the name I had gave my new city. I had been adding on more and more towers and buildings. A little city had grown around the House of Moneekrom. Man, everything had expanded.

I had figured that I might as well give this new city a proper name. So I had picked Harmonee.

The alien metropolis of Harmonee.

And I liked it.

As we hiked along Fordham Road, I kept looking at the addresses and signs on the shops. They had a lot of pizzerias along this street.

"I'm just saying, Lolly," Vega said. "I don't wanna walk in there one day and you *dead*, lying in a big gunky pool of your own blood."

Vega was the crazy one, I thought. Then I saw it across the street. That must'a been it. Vega had stopped blabbering because he had seen it too.

We crossed Fordham Road and stood underneath the big yellow-and-red sign that said BLOCK.

The nightclub beneath the sign hadn't opened yet. It probably wouldn't be open for a few more hours, later tonight. When people would flock in here to drink up and party up. Like Jermaine had done in October.

Block was an ugly place. It wasn't nowhere I would wanna hang out at. I stood there in the cold, inspecting the building for a while. Vega went and fell down on the curb. I sat down beside him and shoved my arms through the sleeves of my parka, zipping it up.

I had got cold all of a sudden.

"This is it, *manin*," I told Vega.

"Yeah, Loll," he said. "I would'a thought they'd shut it down or something. After somebody was murdered up in there."

"I bet if they shut down everywhere in New York where somebody had got smoked, there wouldn't be nowhere left open."

"I'm sorry, Lolly, man."

"Yeah," I said. I felt that rock in my chest grow harder and heavier. "This is it, man. Right here. This is the exact spot!"

The rock got so heavy I couldn't stand it no more. I busted out crying, sitting there on the curb beside Vega.

I didn't know how long I had sat there crying, but after I was done, the rock was gone.

Still, I knew it'd come back.

· ✛ ✛ ·

"Another Lego delivery! Compliments of Yvonne Grayson, Inc.!"

Yvonne shouted almost everything. She was just like Vega when it came to that. She stepped into my bedroom on Saturday and plonked the heavy bag of Legos onto my rug.

"I ought to start charging," Yvonne told me, and flicked the top of my head. It *hurt*.

"Yo, thanks, Yvonne," I said, rubbing my dome.

"You know it's my pleasure, sugar," she said. "You can use these bricks, do something beneficial with them. Besides, Tuttle's would only be trashing them anyways."

"Why they always tossing out so many Legos?" I asked. "It's a *lot*."

Yvonne shrugged. "I guess some of these go out of style and they think it'd be too hard to sell the old ones."

Getting new Legos was a good end to a bad day.

I needed more nights like this.

16

"So let's deconstruct this Bronx trip," Mr. Ali announced all of a sudden. "How did going there make you feel?"

I hesitated. "Sad. *Despondent.*"

Ali nodded. "It was very brave to go there. Knowing how it might affect you."

"I almost expected to see Jermaine standing there in front of Block," I said. "And him telling me and Vega it was all a big joke. I still can't believe he's really gone. It's crazy." I shook my head.

"Did you-all get rid of Jermaine's bed?"

"It's still there. We don't talk about it." I played with one of my shoestrings, twisting it around my little finger.

"Would you like me to talk with your mama about it?" Mr. Ali asked.

I shrugged. "I don't think so. . . ."

"But she knows it's problematic for you, having Jermaine's bed in your room?"

I tilted my head back and opened my mouth toward the ceiling. Mr. Ali was wearing me out.

"It's not problematic, Mr. Ali. I like having his bed in there."

"Lolly, I'm not suggesting that you and your mama forget Jermaine, or leave your memories of him behind. You will always remember him and love him in your heart. But I think you both need to establish a more healthy connection with his memories."

"Building Legos reminds me of him. And, I think, reminds me of my father."

"Your dad's still alive," Ali said, like I didn't know that.

"Yeah, but you know. . ." I had told Ali that Daddy never came around much. Always working, clowning and with his girlfriends. "I was starting to think that building Legos makes me feel like he's still around, still together with my mother. Takes me to that spot a long time ago, you know. When I was little, playing with my Legos in the living room with Daddy and Ma watching over me."

Ali squinted. "Makes sense."

"I feel like Jermaine's there too when I'm building."

"Hold on to those good memories," Mr. Ali said. "Especially those good memories of your brother, Lolly. But you've got to move ahead. Your life is young. Move ahead, brother."

"If I do move ahead, how am I supposed to remember Jermaine?"

Ali thought on this for a minute. "There are ways. Maybe a special possession of his that you can frame and hang on the wall to remember. Or keep a journal of some of his favorite quotes, things he used to say. Understand?"

"I think so," I said.

"Separate the bad emotions from the good memories."

I thought about those thugs at the old barbershop and how they had changed Jermaine. It was hard for me to remember him without including that shop. Like it was tied to him.

Ali smiled at me crooked. Then gave me a corny high five. He glanced at his phone. "It's snack time."

"I'm hungry."

"Me too. Let's break."

17

The alien world of Harmonee was cruising along nicely. The rest of the after-school kids had finally found out about it. Some way, Sunny had got Ms. Jen to confess. I think she tricked our teacher into it. Maybe that girl *would* grow up to be a master investigator, or at least a cop.

Today I had done my homework early again and now was adding on another new Harmonee building, this one created from only red rectangle Legos. This new house was the secret hideout for De-Man.

De-Man was one of my monsters from the Swarm. He had gray, rocky skin.

The Swarm was an interstellar gang of crooks and thugs who harassed folks for no good reason. Except to be ugly.

They had been harassing King Blaze's family for years. The Swarm was the one problem the House of Moneekrom had failed to crack.

So far I had made almost eighty different buildings here

in the storage room, or my city room. I had divided Harmonee into three boroughs, or neighborhoods: the hero borough, the monster borough and the regular borough for all the regular people.

I heard a *ka-klick* behind me. It was the door to the room unlocking and cracking open. Big Rose stuck her big head in through the crack and met eyes with mine.

I froze, holding a few red Legos in my right hand.

Before I could say or do anything, Big Rose had stepped inside, grabbed an armful of Legos and plopped down on the other side of the room, about thirty feet away.

I must'a looked dumb as nuts, squatting there, watching her. She was sitting on the floor with her big fat back to me, building something.

With *my* Legos!

I couldn't believe this girl. I was about to go over there and get a closer angle when she jumped up, flew over toward me again and grabbed another armful of my blocks out of one of the trash bags that Yvonne had gave me.

It went on like this for the next twenty minutes. Her stealing my Legos for whatever she was building over on her side of the room.

She was calm and quiet. I thought about stepping to her, but then I started wondering if she might get mad.

I wasn't scared of her or nothing. We were the same age.

I could box. You couldn't grow up in my hood without learning how to defend yourself.

But also . . . Big Rose was kind of *big*. Way bigger than me. In fact, I started thinking about how in all of my brawls growing up, I had never really got into it with a girl. Or anybody as big as she was.

So I wasn't scared, but I thought maybe I should think about this situation a little more before walking up on her.

The door *ka-klick*ed again. Mr. Ali stuck his head in. His face looked worried, but then, after he saw what was going on, he smirked at me.

"You all cool?" he asked me and Big Head.

She, of course, didn't say nothing.

I shouted across the room to Mr. Ali, "You let her in?"

"That cool with you?" he asked.

I didn't wanna say what I was really thinking, so I just said, "Yeah. It's cool."

He started to close the door.

"She's building with my blocks," I told him. I was starting to feel kind of panicky.

"I *see*," Mr. Ali said back to me. "Very excellent, troops. Stick to it!"

And that was that.

This was how Big Rose invaded Harmonee. I couldn't really gripe to Ali too much. Yeah, they were all my Legos that Yvonne had brought me, but that room didn't really belong to me. It wasn't like Big Rose had broke into my bedroom and just started taking over. Ali had let her in.

The Moneekroms had been invaded by one of the Swarm monsters.

And I didn't like it.

· ✦ ✦ ✦ ·

The days at after-school were kinda tense. Every day I would finish my homework like usual. Big Rose would read her tiny books. And then both of us would wind up building cities in the storage room.

Yeah, she had started building her own city on the opposite side of the room from mines. From what I could tell, hers wasn't anywhere near as nice as Harmonee.

We never spoke and she never asked to use any of my Legos. She just took them. Every now and then Mr. Ali or Ms. Jenna or Sunny or Vega would peek their heads inside to check the progress. All this time, she wasn't saying nothing or even looking at me. All she did was build. And that's all that I did.

Build.

Except now I was feeling different about it. Building Legos wasn't calming me or making me remember good times. I even started having trouble making up new space stories.

Like I said, everything felt hijacked.

Maybe if she had at least *once* brought in some of her own Legos, I wouldn't have minded as much. Maybe if she had just asked at first. Or tried to act thankful.

Her corny buildings were taking away from my own creations. I was glad that Yvonne kept bringing me more Lego trash bags or my production would'a really been slowed down by Rose's thieving.

But one day, I had been working on this new bell tower. It was in the hero borough, and I was almost about to finish it when big fathead Rose came over and tried to grab the last few Legos I had been saving in one of my trash bags.

I saw this and ran over and grabbed the other side of the trash bag.

And the two of us were standing there, both grabbing on to one old trash bag with the last few Legos inside. She would yank the bag toward her, trying to pull it away from me. I would yank back just as drastic.

The whole time, Big Rose was standing there, staring down into the bag. Drooling over those final few Legos, I guess. I pulled the bag back toward me, this time *real* forceful, and she finally jerked her head up and stared at me. *Real* nasty. Like she expected me to back down.

I didn't.

I glared back at her. We stood there, eyeball to eyeball.

I loaded into my stare all the evilness, all the viciousness, I had felt since that night on Halloween. That rock that had been living inside my chest boiled so hot it melted and shot at her like lasers out of my eye sockets.

I guess Rose felt the burn. She dropped the trash bag like it was hot.

I watched her sit down with her back against the wall near her little city. Her face was tight. Her eyes had got red. Her chest was pumping. She stuck her head between her legs and stayed like that.

Just the two of us in this big room that felt too small. I had felt like a champ after staring her down. Now I didn't feel as big as all that.

I dropped the Lego bag in front of her. But grabbed out one brick for myself, just to let her know what was up, and left the rest of them for Big Rose.

I snapped my one brick into place on the building I had been working on.

On the other side of the room, I heard those other bricks click and clack together, sounding like money. I knew she had reached her hand inside to pull out the last ones.

18

By the next day, I had a fresh supply of Legos, and I knew how to get rid of big-head Rose.

I had been watching her build. She was fast, but still learning. I'd been messing with Legos for years. A lot of the mistakes I had seen her make over the past days were mistakes I used to make when I first started.

I would take her down hard.

Me just thinking that made me feel good. Well, maybe not *good*, exactly. "Good" ain't the right word.

It made me feel different.

Ever since Halloween, I'd noticed that taking my revenge on other people would do something to that rock I'd been feeling in my chest. Being evil wouldn't make the rock disappear. But being that way did make me not mind the rock being there.

Just like when I heard the other after-schoolers make fun of Rose and call her names. Or when I called her names. Or when I told Heike there was a mouse.

All that made me not mind the rock. Making Rose feel bad made those feelings inside of me feel harder, less like a real person.

And there was something else inside of me that was afraid of that. Afraid of me becoming more and more . . .

Bad thoughts.

Big Head was on her side of the room building some lopsided wall.

"Rosamund!" I shouted.

She glanced at me over her shoulder.

"Come here," I said.

She ignored me. I stomped over to her. I watched what the girl was doing for a minute, then squatted.

"Big Rose, this storage room ain't big enough for the two of us," I said all low, just in case Mr. Ali was eavesdropping outside the door. She just kept on stacking blocks. "I know you can hear me," I told her. "You ain't dumb like you like everybody to think." She paused. "I see you reading your little books every day."

Big Rose turned, but avoided my face.

"This is *my* storage room," I whispered. "It was *my* idea to ask Ali if I could use it. These is *my* blocks."

She blinked.

"But I can see you are the sort that won't bail unless they're forced out." I leaned in toward her. "You ain't the only *gangsta* up in here."

I was feeling bad as Tupac.

She started stacking blocks again. I grabbed her hand to stop her. She jerked her hand away.

I looked toward the door for Mr. Ali, then went on, "Now, this is how it's gonna go down, *Biggie*. You and me, we gonna have a contest. Got it? A *contest*." I stood up because my knees were starting to hurt.

Big Rose surprised me by standing up too. I didn't like this because now she towered over me. She must'a been at least half a foot taller. I folded my arms and tried to look tough. I had learned that this was the only way to deal with this one.

Big Rose folded her arms too and glared down at me.

"Um," I said. "So this is how it goes: You know that big green dragon down at Tuttle's Toys? Their Midtown store?"

Big Rose nodded and started staring at the floor.

"That dragon is maybe twenty feet high, at *least*, and it's made all out of Legos. Probably a gazillion tiny Lego bricks. In fact, the dude who built that dragon is probably a Lego *master*. The way I see it, only a Lego master belongs here in my city room."

I waved my hands around me, the way Mr. Jonathan would'a done. Big Rose just kept on staring at the floor. I guessed she was listening.

Now I said, not whispering no more, "You and me are gonna have a contest to see who can build the tallest tower here in my city room. A tower made out of Legos. We start tomorrow during after-school. The first one of us to stack a tower that is ten feet tall is the winner! The loser is banished from my city room forever."

I stuck my hand out toward her. She waited a minute, then shook it. Big Rose had a sturdy grip. She still wasn't looking me in the face.

But this girl did not know who she was dealing with.

Rookie, I thought. *I am the true Lego master.* I grinned at her as evilly as I could.

On the first day of our Ten-Foot Tower Contest, Big Rose was first into my city room. By the time I had finished the decimals that Ms. Ling had assigned, Big Rose had already laid the first story of her tower.

She didn't even meet eyes with me when I stepped into the room.

I could tell that she was taking this contest serious. Didn't want to get booted out of my Lego Universe, my Lego-verse.

I had borrowed Ma's tape measurer from her closet so we could keep track of our towers' heights. I knew Big Rose would never be able to make something go as tall as ten feet high. She didn't have the skills.

She wasn't no Lego master.

Dummy.

I got busy building.

We had a lot of blocks, but I had guessed each of us might have to start tearing apart bits of our cities in order to build our towers as high as we both needed to. We hadn't reached that point yet, but we might.

I decided to call mine Blaze Tower. After King Blaze, the ruler of my kingdom. Blaze Tower was where the monarch went to be alone with his thoughts about the galaxy and when he wanted to deep-think.

Instead of ten feet, Blaze Tower was really ten miles high, I thought. I stared up at the storage-room ceiling and up through it. I imagined the clouds and stars up above. Something ten miles high might stick up into outer space.

It would be a miracle building that everybody would admire and get jealous of.

The second day of the contest I had decided that I would really go crazy. I had made progress with my tower, but it seemed like as fast as I piled bricks, Big Rose was always a little faster.

I wasn't worried about her, really. She couldn't keep up that pace. She was still a rookie. I was the starter.

I hadn't told nobody about me and Big Rose's bet. I had

thought about telling, but then I had thought about how it might form a crowd in here. This thing made me anxious enough without having all of after-school ogling over my shoulders.

At the end of the second contest day, I took out Ma's tape measurer and recorded what we had done so far. Big Rose's construction was almost four feet tall. Blaze Tower was just under three feet.

She didn't react to this news. Just grabbed her stack of tiny books and flew.

I was hoping now that I could catch up to her. Big Rose's tower was about two feet taller than mine was. I could not let her whup me. This was *my* city room.

King Blaze was the ruler.

Today, the third day of the Ten-Foot Tower Contest, I was feeling edgy. Vega and Sunnshyne sat on the floor, munching granola bars, watching us build.

Big Rose had got to the point where she had to use one of the ladders in here to reach the top of her tower. And she had started cannibalizing parts of her city to add on to its height.

My Blaze Tower had made progress, but it was still behind hers.

I had started to get a little worried.

I would not let this dumb girl succeed, I thought.

I usually liked a good test. I think Ma had got me hooked growing up because we used to compete with each other on a lot of things. She was always pinning me down and wrestling me. . . .

My favorite was our story challenges. Those things were fun.

How you played it was easy. Ma and me would lie on her bed and she would start reading out loud from one of her mystery books. Usually Sherlock Holmes, but sometimes other ones.

At a certain part of the book, she would stop reading and she would turn to me. "What you think, Lolly?" Ma'd say. "What do you *think*?"

Then I would take over the story from out of my head. I would just make up what happened next and tell her out loud. After a while, she would take her turn, picking up where I'd left off, and she'd make up some new part of the story.

We'd go back and forth like that, adding on, until Ma would say it was time for bed.

I would always get the chance to end the story. I loved that. Those story challenges were fun. We needed to start playing them again.

On her side of the room, Biggie was still working real

fast. I didn't think she ever got tired. I didn't know you could stack Legos as quick as she was doing.

I needed to hurry.

The fourth day smelled like death.

Defeat.

The night before, I had measured the heights. Hers was almost nine feet. Mine was almost seven.

We were both standing on ladders now. On opposite sides of the room. Big Rose was still laying bricks as fast as she could. I was too.

And the vultures were dangling around. For some wacko reason, Ms. Jenna had started to let our after-school class come to the storage room after they had finished their homework.

Everybody was lying around, watching me compete with Big Rose and adding comments about who they thought would win. They even ate their snacks in here. It was like a dang party.

The chance of Big Rose winning scared me. I really didn't want to let her win and for me to get banished from my own city room in front of everybody. It might could happen.

I started wondering if Big Rose would want to call off this game. Maybe come to a truce or something.

Nah.

I wouldn't give up, I decided. If this girl was better than me, she was gonna have to prove it. Run the clock down all the way to the end.

Ten miles into the sky!

We had both used up Legos from whole sections of our cities. I had torn apart and recycled some of the blocks from Victarea and Hypozmia, two of my neighborhoods. I really hadn't wanted to do that.

And my shoulders had started hurting. Real bad. I climbed up to the next step of my ladder so I could reach the top of Blaze Tower. And started layering on another story of bricks.

I chewed on a chocolate Sunny gave me for energy.

Ms. Jen, gnawing on one of her pink fingernails, watched me.

Across the room I saw Big Rose shuffle down to the floor from the top of her ladder. She rushed toward her own city and started pulling apart more blocks to use on her tower.

I got to say I was impressed. Even if I thought she was using too many larger Legos on top of her tower and lots of small ones on the bottom. It had held up good.

Yesterday I was watching her creation and I thought that it looked familiar. I had seen it somewhere before, but couldn't remember where.

Big Rose was constructing an actual building from real

life, I realized. I searched, and shook my head after I had found a pic of the building on my phone.

One World Trade Center. The tallest building in America. I could only shake my head again.

Now I watched her gather up more bricks and stomp back toward her ladder. I really was starting to feel defeated. . . . I wondered if . . .

Just then, that loud familiar sound began to rumble the room. It had been making that same noise since the first day I had started building my castle in here.

The big heating vent on the wall was starting to shoot out warm air. But the huge vent was blowing right at the top of Big Rose's Freedom Tower. Today was the first day that her building had been tall enough to reach the vent.

The whole room watched her tower for a minute.

It was starting to twitch.

Back and forth. Back, back. Forth, forth.

From on top my ladder, I stared down at Big Rose. Her mouth hung open. She watched her tower wobble more and more and more and more!

"It's wiggling!" Darrell B. shouted.

"Oh no," Ms. Jen said. She covered her eyes.

It wouldn't be long now.

And sure enough, her creation tilted just a little too much to one side and sailed downward in a *fabuloso* explosion of

Legos. Everybody jumped back. Not only had her Freedom Tower collapsed, but when it did fall, it fell right on top of the rest of her city.

Lego bricks skittered across the floor.

Big Rose was obliterated. Her face got real red. She shut her eyes.

"I win! I win!" I shouted from on top my ladder. I was so joyous I shot up into the air. When I landed back onto the ladder's step, one of my feet slipped.

Seven feet in the air, I almost fell off my ladder. My right hand snatched the ladder. My left hand swung out into the air. It scraped Blaze Tower.

"Oh!" I yelled.

My Blaze Tower didn't fall. I had caught it with my left hand and was holding it still. I carefully steadied both feet onto the ladder. Trying not to shake, I kept holding on to my tower.

"Lolly, let go and come down," Ms. Jen said.

I didn't wanna speak, out of fear that the sound might crumble my building. Though I was safe on the ladder again, I was afraid to let go of my tower. I didn't want it to start wobbling. I heard somebody cackle.

It was Big Rose down below. She had run over to me and was standing down below with the gladdest face.

"Help!" I finally said. Nobody knew what to do. I kept holding on to my tower to keep it steady. "Help me, Vega!"

He scratched his head.

Big Rose grinned and shrugged.

There really was nothing they could do. There wasn't any way they could help me. I must'a stood there for at least fifteen minutes, one hand grabbing my ladder, the other hand gripping the top of Blaze Tower.

My shoulders and arms ached.

Big Rose was now sitting on the floor, legs crossed, smiling up at me.

"Come down, Lolly," Ms. Jen said again. "Your tower's steady."

I closed my eyes, tense. My left hand released my building. Blaze Tower seemed okay. I was relieved.

But then I noticed it was actually twitching the tiniest bit.

Side to side.

I kept reaching out to touch it, trying to make it steady. But every time I tapped its side, that made the tremble worse. It was swooping now, back and forth.

Back and forth. Back, back. Forth, forth.

The crumble started at the foot of the tower. The bottom skidded to one side like somebody had kicked its legs out from under it. Then the top of the tower leaned and tipped over and my dreams of becoming the Lego master of the city room came crashing down.

"No!" I yelled, and shut my eyes. *"Blaze."*

Everybody hopped back some more. Once the tinkling of the last brick had stopped echoing in the room, I gazed around. It looked like a Lego giant had just thrown up in here.

"What is going on?" I heard Mr. Ali shout. He stood in the doorway, gawking at the mess.

I didn't have nothing to say. In a funny way, my tower collapse seemed to ease me up a bit, soften my chest rock. I didn't know why.

"Wallace," Ali said, "I think it's time we had another chat."

After that, the only thing I could hear was Big Rose's loud handclaps and giggles repeating across the room. Her face was lit up.

Delighted.

19

The next Saturday morning Vega and me ran over to the rec center on 134th to play some ball. I sometimes hated hooping with Vega because he always liked to check too hard, but when *you* checked *him* he would start whining.

Like a big baby.

And when he lost, he was too much. He would act like everything in the world had depended on him owning you in that game. He always took it too serious.

So I had let him win today.

After ball, while we were walking home, Vega started to ask me about Big Rose. It had been weeks since she had rushed into my space and started looting my Legos. Just this week, we had both watched our towers explode in our faces.

Even though Blaze Tower had stood a little longer than her Freedom Tower, neither one of us had reached ten feet high. I had probably won our contest because mine had stood a few minutes longer, but hers had been taller than mines before that air vent blew it down. I couldn't tell if either one of us had won, really.

We were both still building in the city room.

The mood between us was not as nervous as it had been. In fact, she had actually started to mutter things at me every now and then.

Not full sentences. Just words that I could barely hear.

So she did speak!

"A mysterious mystery," Vega said, all solemn.

We had traveled down to 130th Street and had started to cut over west across Harlem. Standing on the sidewalk was this dude in a navy-blue suit and holding a leather bag. His suit even had a vest, but that was dark gray. He checked his phone and smiled at me and Vega.

"Hey, now," he said. We nodded.

Just then, this black sports car zoomed up. There was this fine female driving. He gave her a kiss and they sped off together.

I wondered where they were going.

Vega and me kept walking and talking. He dribbled my basketball between his legs and fumbled it every few steps. Once, the ball even bounced into the middle of the street. A big red Hummer swerved out of the way, though, and cursed at us before speeding off.

After Vega ran out and got my ball, I snatched it from

him and shot him a grimy look. We strolled on, to another block, before he had something else to say.

"Why don't you kick her out?" he asked me.

"Big Rose?" I said. "How am I gonna kick her out of somewhere that don't even belong to me?"

"They're your bricks."

"Ali wouldn't like that. It was him that sent her in there. I don't know why. But if I piss Ali off, he might not let me build in the storage room no more."

Vega rubbed his forehead and watched the sun. It was beaming, one of them freaky warm days in late winter.

"Why is it so hot?" he asked. "We just got out of February!"

"Yeah," I said. "Let's cross."

We sprinted across the avenue and hopped over the median. On the other side, there was a bodega on the corner with a crowd of older boys hanging out front. My eyeballs searched the mob for enemies, but didn't find none.

Two of the boys out front were selling. One of them sat on a fire hydrant spitting lyrics:

If they bury me, no need to worry
I expect retaliation in a hurry

Old-school Tupac Shakur, I thought, listening to that dude. Jermaine used to say that listening to Tupac was like listening in on the mind of every young Black man in the ghetto. I didn't used to believe that.

"You think you'd ever join a gang?" I asked my friend after we'd left those dudes behind.

"Me? And get shot? What good is that? Mami would be so sad. But probably not my cousin Frito. I don't even like guns. Would you join?"

"I like doing stuff my own way too much to join up. If you're in a crew, you got to do what the crew say, and I don't do what other people say. Unless it's Ma. Or Daddy. Or Yvonne."

Vega laughed at me. "Or your shrink, Mr. Ali," he said. "With that face, he's more scary than Yvonne. Yo, I wish my mami had a dope girlfriend that brought me gifts all the time!"

"What?!" I asked. "You wish your ma was gay?"

Vega laughed.

I remembered something all of a sudden. "Vega, I know what she's up to."

"My mami?"

"Nah, dummy. Big Rose."

"You think she's cutting up body parts?"

"I know what she's *building*. What is wrong with you, man? She is building an exact copy, a small Lego version of St. Nick Houses. Where we live."

His eyes grew wide.

"Yep," I went on.

"It's probably a map of where she buried the bodies," he said.

I ignored this. "She ain't done yet, but so far she has copied every little detail of the development and built it into her city."

"You mean *your* city, man," Vega said. "They're still your blocks. Yvonne brings them for you, not that big-head girl."

"I know. But I gotta admit, I am a little impressed with her construction skills. She ain't no joke. And it's different having somebody else in there with me, even though she stays on the other side of the room working on her stuff. I kinda feel like we're working on something together."

We had been just about to tromp onto St. Nick Houses property, but Vega froze on the sidewalk. I kept on and glanced behind at him.

I saw Concrete hovering in the courtyard. A dozen cops had rolled up on Concrete and he was trying to talk his way out of there. I decided to avoid them.

Vega caught up with me. He was grinning like a idiot.

"You're in love with a ugly girl," he told me. He busted out laughing. "I just realized."

"It ain't even like that, man," I said. "You ain't got no sense. I don't even like that Frankenstein. She is a monster."

I couldn't believe how clueless Vega could get.

"Wait," he said. "Ain't that your *other* girlfriend, Sunny? And April E.?"

I looked where he was pointing and saw the two girls hiding behind a big tree on one of the grassy parts of St. Nick. It was hard to tell who they was hiding from, but it wasn't me and Vega. They hadn't seen us yet.

Before we could yell at them, they both ran off in the other direction, and disappeared around a corner.

"You see that?" Vega said.

After we went over to where they had been hiding, we didn't uncover nothing there. But Vega found an old cardboard box, sitting upside down, about twenty feet away.

This box was actually *moving.* It slid across the grass from the left to the right and then back to the left. It was hard to tell if the wind had been moving it or if it had been moving by itself.

Vega punted the cardboard box. A skinny red chicken flapped out from under it. The chicken flipped around. Pecked at us. And blasted off when Vega tried to grab it. The angry red bird was too fast and ducked beneath some bushes beside building 9400.

We gave up and headed toward our building's lobby.

In the elevator up, both of us were quiet, trying to figure

out what we had just seen. Finally, just before we got off on the seventh floor, Vega said, "I guess those girls weren't joking about being detectives."

He busted out laughing again before we dipped inside my crib for some fruit pops and video games.

20

Here in our city room over the past few weeks, one of the cities had been copied and another city had evolved.

I say "evolved" because that's the only way to describe mine. My buildings and city plans sprang out of my head. I just built this stuff and tried not to think about where it came from. Like I was actually making up hip-hop lyrics or something.

My city was about twenty feet around its borders and growing. Rose's was way smaller than mine, but she spent more time adding real-life details to hers.

I guess Rose and me had evolved too. We had started to communicate.

Over the weeks, we had started to share with each other what we were doing. Share ideas.

She would sometimes quit what she was doing and stroll over to watch what I was building. I sometimes did the same.

The week after our contest bombed, Mr. Ali and me had gone outside to the St. Nick courtyard. It was a wide round space surrounded by benches and sprinkled with trees.

The weather wasn't so bad that day, so we ate our snack out there and talked. I tore apart the bread from my cheese sandwich to feed the black and gray squirrels.

Ali asked me a question. "So you don't mind it? Her building in the storage room with you?"

"Does it make a difference?" I asked.

"Everything makes a difference," he said. "Life's all about differences and choices. I'm just glad you two haven't killed each other in there."

I grinned at that. "It ain't terrible. I still want back my space."

"You know, Rose needs space too." He didn't say nothing for a while. "When you deal with her, be patient. Girls like Big Rose, you know, just because they don't smile at first, that doesn't mean they aren't friendly." I squinted at Mr. Ali. "Be patient and keep trying to connect because it takes her a little longer to pick up on what you're meaning to say . . . socially and body language and all that. Understand?"

I nodded.

"Emotions can be tricky for somebody like her," he said. One of the squirrels grabbed a edge of bread and ran under a bench with it. "How you and *your* emotions getting along?" Mr. Ali asked. "Those bad thoughts you always talk about?"

I didn't say nothing. Ali stared up at the tall development buildings surrounding us on all sides. He squinted at the top of one of them, like he was remembering something.

"You aren't the only one with bad thoughts, young man," Mr. Ali said. "Be grateful you got what you got."

I didn't know what he was talking about. Up until now my life hadn't seemed like anything to be grateful for.

My eyes followed his to the building he was staring at. It was just one of the regular old thirteen project buildings that made up St. Nick.

They were all just bricks and blocks.

Today, watching Rose finish up her Lego model of where we lived, I was still wondering what Ali had meant. Sometimes he didn't make any sense.

Now that Rose had completed her little version of our housing development, she had moved on to copying some of the other buildings that surrounded it. I didn't know how she remembered how all of them looked and how she got them so exact.

It was like a touchable map of our neighborhood. She had built miniature versions of the Schomburg Center, Harlem YMCA and other stuff.

This afternoon Mr. Ali and Ms. Jenna brought our after-school group into the storage room so everybody could snoop at our progress. Rose and me had done a lot of repair work after the great tower quakes.

I had also asked Ali if I could try out my Maestro game on them. It was something I had invented, a game you could play by using my Harmonee city like a 3-D board game.

Our after-school class came shuffling in.

They walked around the edges of Harmonee. I explained the hero and monster boroughs to them all. I also told them the story behind the Moneekrom family I had made up.

They listened, mostly.

It was cool.

Most of them liked my city the best, I think, but Quintesha and Darrell B. hung out around Rose's little St. Nick PJs. They couldn't believe she had built it. They kept asking her questions. She would answer with one or two words, not looking them in the eye. She even managed to smile once, just for a half a second. You *did* have to be patient with Rose. And it helped to not ask too many questions. Asking her too many questions—even if they were like, "How you doing?"—would shut her down.

All my afterschool seemed to love my Maestro game.

Maestro was something I had come up with when I had started rebuilding my city again. The game was named after this space dude that I had created called the Maestro. He had lightning eyes, and was not a hero or monster but lived on an island off the coast of Victarea, the hero borough.

Way before, Ms. Jen and me had written all of these word and math problems down on a deck of index cards. To play, you had to roll your dice and move your big game piece across these grids I had built all across Harmonee.

For the game pieces, I used a bunch of old action figures I had found in the after-school toy basket.

I divided the kids up into either heroes or monsters. They all took turns rolling the dice and moving their pieces through the squares in different parts of Harmonee.

If you landed on a Lego grid that had a trap on it—quicksand, falling rocks or lava—you had to pull one of the index cards and correctly answer that question for points or you died.

The team with the most points, or who reached Maestro Island first, won. But if you reached Maestro Island first, you had a whole new, tougher set of questions to answer before you'd defeat the Maestro.

Sunny screeched after she first moved her piece.

I had gave her the monster Worsa the War Witch. In my head, Worsa had green skin and wore a cool red hood, but for my game here I had picked out an old Black Barbie doll—the best I could do.

Sunny rolled her dice and landed in a pool of lava. After doing that, she had five minutes to solve a math problem or her character would die.

She died.

Poor Worsa.

Ms. Jen said maybe I should give the kids ten minutes

to solve a math problem instead of just five. I told her I'd consider it.

These kids needed to learn more.

While most of the after-school was huddled around the borders of Harmonee, playing Maestro, I stepped over to Rose, who had leaned against the far wall with her arms folded.

"They like our cities," I told her.

"Yes," Rose said.

"We gotta keep constructing, then," I said.

She nodded up and down super fast. "They like your game," she said. Rose wiped her nose with the back of her hand and watched me grab a book out of my orange backpack.

"I never showed you this before, but we talked about it," I said, handing her the heavy hardback. She took it gently in her hands, staring down at the cover.

"*A Pattern of Architecture,*" she read out loud. "*World's Greatest Marvels.*"

"Yeah, that's the Christmas present my man Steve gave me."

She nodded fast. "I know," she said. "It looks good."

"Yeah. I'm catching the train down to Midtown this Saturday. To try and find some of those buildings in there. I'm gonna explore buildings. Since you like 'em too, you wanna come? You could help me find 'em."

Rose studied the book's photo of the Lipstick Building for a long time, then just nodded her head real fast again without looking up.

"Oh, cool. I didn't think you'd want to. Okay, we'll meet at the four train on Saturday."

But before I could speak anything else, another girl's voice said something from behind me. "You never ask me to do nothing outside of after-school, Lolly," the voice said.

I turned around. It was Sunny standing there with April E. right behind her.

"Huh?" I said.

"Oh, you're just stupid . . . childish . . . ," Sunny shouted. "Dumb *coconut.*"

She squinted her eyes at me and then at Rose. Rose glared back at her and let out one big laugh. Sunny was out of there before I could even say anything.

I felt sorry for Sunny.

I didn't know why.

Today was Yvonne's day off.

While she was waiting for Ma to come home from work, Vega and me convinced her to walk us down to the game store on 125th Street. She agreed, and right when she had agreed, I knew that I would get her to buy me a video game for my new system.

Yvonne was easy to talk into stuff. I think she thought that doing me favors would make my mother love her more.

At the store, we browsed around a bit. Vega and me kept bringing Yvonne all of the brand-new games that had just come out. She would grab the box, flip it over, read the price tag and toss the box back onto the shelf.

After a while, though, she decided to buy me two games from the used bin. I let Vega pick them since he would be the one playing them the most. Just as we were leaving the shop, Yvonne got a message from my mother.

"Come on, boys," she told us, reading her phone. "We meeting Sue-ellen at Applebee's. I'm treating you to dinner."

I loved Applebee's.

And Yvonne loved taking us there. I liked it because it was like a real restaurant where a waiter would come to your table and ask you what you wanted. It was a special deal to go there for us.

Waiting in a booth at the restaurant, Yvonne, Vega and me ordered some sodas and French fries to pass the time until Ma came. I knew when she did finally get here, she would be starving from standing on her feet all day doing security.

"Your moms tell me you gonna hang out with that girl this weekend," Yvonne said to me out of nowhere.

I shrugged and sipped on my orange soda. I tried not to

look at Vega. I felt his eyes all over me. Instead, I inspected a paper leprechaun that was dangling from the ceiling on a string.

A chilly draft blew in through the open door. Though it was March, it had gotten crazy cold again outside.

"You mean Sunnshyne Dixon-Knight?" Vega asked Yvonne, all loud. "Or did you mean Big Rose? That one's Lolly's true *novia*. They going to get married in their storage closet and have big-head, special babies."

Vega laughed. Pepsi spurted out his nostrils.

"Vega!" Yvonne shouted. She handed him a napkin. He kept laughing. Yvonne raised one of her thin eyebrows at me. "Is she your girl? Inquiring minds want to know," she asked.

"Yeah, Loll!" Vega said, giggling.

I slapped him on the back of his neck and we started wrestling there in the booth.

21

It wasn't as chilly as it had been.

I was glad because we'd probably be spending most of the morning and afternoon outside. I was still sleepy. I probably would'a overslept, but the sound of a chicken crowing had raised me up early.

I guessed that skinny red chicken was still running around St. Nick somewhere.

His crowing at the break of dawn had woke Ma up too. Like most Saturdays, she would be working the whole day in Brooklyn. I liked this because with her being gone all Saturday, I could usually do whatever I wanted without her telling me not to.

Her day at work was my day to be free.

Explore.

Somebody groaned behind me. I turned to watch this Spanish dude stand near a wall, with his knees bent, staring off into space. Every now and then he would act like he would need to sit down, but then he would just stay standing, dazed.

He was in his world. Built out of drugs. Who knew how long he'd be there like that, not knowing who he was.

I was on the corner at 125th and Lexington in Harlem. This place had to be the most psycho corner in all of New York City.

It *had* to be.

Daddy Rachpaul had told me that the reason this corner was so nuts was that all different types of people met here. Added on to the ex-cons living in halfway houses around the way, there were the addicts who used the drug clinics nearby. Also there were city buses that stopped at this corner to take people to homeless shelters.

So all these unlucky people mixed up together is what made this place kind of funky.

"Yo, youngblood!" somebody called. "I'm talking to you, brother!"

I met eyes with this old dude wearing only a stained blue windbreaker. Yeah, it was warmer today than it had been, but not warm enough to just be wearing an old dirty windbreaker. It must'a been about forty degrees.

"What's up," I said to the dude. My eyes started scanning the crowds of people rushing past. Most of them were racing down into the subway station, trying to get somewhere else.

"Spare a dollar?" Windbreaker asked me. "I'm trying to buy a coffee."

I handed him the change in my pocket with: "That's all I got."

"Youngblood, God bless you," he mumbled, then bowed and skidded off.

Again I peeped at the time on my phone. It was way past ten a.m. I was getting tired of waiting. I stashed my phone in the back pocket of my jeans.

"Youngblood!" somebody called out.

For a second I thought it was old Windbreaker, back for more coffee money. But after thinking for that second, my brain realized it couldn't have been him back. This new voice was different.

Young.

I turned toward the voice and that heavy stone plopped right back onto my heart. I was staring that dude Harp right in the face. One of the older boys who had been following me since Christmas Eve.

I didn't say nothing, but turned to run.

Gully was standing right in my way, though. Out of nowhere. He mean-mugged me, then glanced at the people all around us.

"Come here, little man," Gully said to me, almost whispering. His stank breath was all up in my face. He had had an egg sandwich for breakfast, I could tell.

The two boys grabbed an arm each and toted me around the corner to 124th Street. I started kicking. There weren't as many people here. Almost nobody this Saturday morning.

"You look *skeered*, little man," Gully told me. He shoved me over to Harp, who grabbed me by my backpack before I could take off. "What's your name?"

I didn't say nothing.

"We know who you is, *Lollypop*," Harp said into my ear. He made a popping sound with his lips. "You hang with them Dominicans over in St. Nick. What you doing over on the *East* Side this morning?"

"On 125th?" Gully said.

"He a quiet little mouse," Harp said.

Gully cracked a smile. "You wander down to this part of East 125th, you got to pay the fare, Lollypop," he said. "You know the rules." He stepped closer. "Gimme that phone."

I didn't move, and Gully's eyes got all narrow. He wasn't mad. It seemed like he wasn't sure if I had understood.

"That phone in your back pocket," Gully said. "Harper and me could just grab it, but we want you to give it to us. As a *gift*. We don't want there to be no misunderstanding about it. It's just like you giving us your phone because we are really, really tight."

"*Best* friends," Harp whispered.

I could feel my heartbeat in my ears. I knew they was

going to have my phone. That wasn't really what made me sizzle. The sad, angry thing was that there was nothing I could do to stop them.

There were two of them. They were both bigger. Like Ma always said, I had skinny-boy muscles.

Gully stuck his finger in my face. "Give it up, Lollypop."

I turned away.

And saw Big Rose stomp around the corner.

Lips tucked, she was skipping in that way that she always did. Real fast, so that her big head bobbed up into the air every time she took a step. With both hands, she was clutching a plastic lunch box against her chest.

I heard her say, "When you die, they bury you."

Looking confused, Harp glanced at her. Rose was moving so fast toward me and the boys that I didn't even have time to warn her to hold back. I didn't want her to get hurt.

Right after that thought flew through my brain cells, I watched Rose raise her lunch box above her head and then—*blaap!*

She had whopped Gully so hard on the back of his head that her lunch box broke in two. Food went flying out. Gully stumbled forward onto me, drooling, and we both tumbled to the cement. I scraped my hand trying to keep from falling.

By the time I looked up at Rose and Harp, I saw him ducking away from her, trying to get some distance between his head and her heavy fists. She was pummeling Harp's head like a jackhammer breaking concrete.

One fist after another fist flew out and landed on Harp's head, eye, nose or neck before he had any chance to react. Not only was Big Rose taller than both Harp and Gully, but she carried more weight on her than those boys, who were probably two years older.

I jumped up and lunged toward Harp.

Leaving his friend Gully still dazed on the sidewalk, Harp took off running east on 124th Street. Rose threw her Red Delicious apple after him as he ran. It just missed his head.

Both of us turned to glare down at Gully, who was trying to stand.

Before I could say anything, Rose ran at him with the hard metal thermos that had also been flung out of her broken lunch box. She didn't smack him with it, but stood there, waiting.

Gully stumbled backward out of her reach. His eyes narrowed again, just like they had narrowed at me before, right after I'd refused to hand him my phone.

He looked like he didn't understand how this had happened to him. How this girl had smashed out him and his roughneck partner. For a second, I thought he'd forgot how to speak, until he unloaded the longest stretch of curse words at Rose that I'd ever heard anybody gush out.

Rose let out a scream and raised her thermos higher above her head.

Like she was about to dunk it against Gully's brains.

Still cursing, Gully tore off in the opposite direction. When Rose tried to follow, I was just able to hold her back. After she had finished puffing, we picked up what was left of her lunch off the street and made it back to the subway at 125th and Lex.

The McDonald's restaurant we went to in Midtown Manhattan for lunch was so crowded we had to locate a corner booth on the second floor upstairs. I was glad because from the second floor you could watch all the people racing and rushing down below.

Rose wasn't tired, but I was. We had spent most of the afternoon hunting all around Midtown for famous buildings that were in my architects book.

I treated Rose to lunch. All she had wanted was chicken nuggets and apple slices. I guessed it was my fault that she had had to wreck her own lunch by pounding Gully upside his ugly head with it.

"That boy pointed in your face," she told me. "He shouldn't do that."

I decided to never stick my finger in her face.

This Rose was *okay*, I thought.

We both sat up there eating and looking out. I took a chew out of my double cheeseburger and reached for my phone. I had bagged pictures of all the different buildings Rose and me had spotted.

"Here's the Chippendale Building," I said, showing her. "That was the first one we found. Designed by Philip Johnson and John Burgee."

She nodded, and spoke with mashed-up chicken in her mouth. "Fifty-Fifth and Madison."

I thumbed a page in my book. "It says it's nicknamed the Chippendale Building because it looks like a piece of furniture. *Huh!*"

"What?" Rose asked.

"That's what it says. The top of the building is built like the top of a old cabinet."

We went on like that for a while, eating and talking about what we had seen that day. My favorite was the Chrysler Building. To me, it was a building from another planet. Rose's was some building we had explored at 300 West 57th Street. It took a minute for me to figure out that she had meant that Hearst building.

It was weird and shiny. Well, the top was. The bottom was old stone.

Rose was always so exact in how she talked. When she talked about a building, she didn't say, "You know, the big one shaped like a tube of lipstick." Instead, she would say, "The oval-shaped reddish orange one at Fifty-Third and Third Avenue."

This girl was different, but that's nothing new. I was a little different too, I had come to realize over the past few months. I mean, how many grown kids spend all their free time building Lego cities in dusty old storage rooms?

"Hey, Rose," I started, "what makes you so different?"

She shrugged and slid my book across the table toward herself.

"You know," I said. "I mean, you like to be by yourself so much. You got a solid memory too. Real solid. Is that because you're homeschooled? You gonna build all the buildings we saw today? In our city room?"

She nodded, eyes down in the book.

"All that, from memory?" I asked.

She nodded again, flipping a page.

I whistled. "I couldn't do that, man. That's why I took pictures." I sipped the last of my orange drink. I noticed the sound of the straw slurping made her frown, so I cut it out.

Rose said, still frowning, "I'm not autistic."

Her head jerked toward the sound of a chair leg screeching across the floor. An Asian family that had been sitting next to us was leaving.

"I'm not autistic," she said again.

"I know. You ain't got no definition," I said.

She nodded and turned a page without meeting eyes with me.

"Well, I always feel different from everybody else," I said. "It gets worse the more old I get, I think. Just between you and me, I wasn't doing too good over the holidays. I hated the holidays. I felt like I was gonna die."

Rose glanced at me and asked, "Why were you going to die?"

She grinned and dove back down into my book. I peeked around to see if anybody was listening. Everybody else was all in their own other worlds. Two Black women dressed in short skirts sat down where the Asians had sat.

"I had started to think about doing bad stuff. Like how I treated you. Last October, on Halloween, my brother Jermaine died," I told Rose. "Actually, he didn't just die. Some thug shot him at a nightclub up in the Bronx. They haven't found him yet—the dude that shot my brother—but I know he's still out there."

On the street below, some fat cop was giving some delivery van a ticket. The driver was trying to talk his way out of it. The cop just walked away.

I sighed. "The storage room, Harmonee, working on our two cities . . . it helps. I still think about doing bad things sometimes. I'm not completely better, but I feel like I could be better."

"I'm better," Rose said. Without taking her eyes out of *A Pattern of Architecture*, she said, "August sixteenth my mother jumped from the top of building number 9900."

"Oh, man!" I said. All the buildings in St. Nick were fourteen stories tall. I knew firsthand from sitting on top of mine flying paper planes. "Rose, man, I'm sorry."

"I'm better," she said again.

I thought back to last summer and remembered what she was talking about. At first, the cops had tried to keep the jumper's name quiet, but soon everybody was talking about the lady who jumped. I couldn't remember her name. . . .

"Desirée Green," Rose said.

"Yeah, I remember, Rose," I said. "Oh, man!"

Rose's last name was different, probably her father's last name. And mostly her grandmother had raised her, she told me, since her own mother had never been around.

I remembered all that and everybody in St. Nick being so sad about it, that woman killing herself like that right in our home. Rose said her mother didn't grow up in St. Nick and never really visited Rose's grandma Betty much.

Man!

Then, out of nowhere, she started to kick her leg back and forth. With her eyes on the floor, she told me, "'Rosamund, when you die, they bury you, but your soul flies to the stars.'"

Her leg stopped. She stared back into my book.

I didn't know what she had meant. What she had said wasn't in the book. She had said the same stuff to Harp and Gully this morning.

I sat there watching her read until she said she had to go home. Her gran would get worried.

As we headed toward the subway to go back up to Harlem, I scoped out the tall Midtown skyscrapers one last time. The idea of falling from, or jumping from, the roof of my own building used to scare me. I couldn't help but think about what it would be like to fall from the top of one of these mile-high skyscrapers here, down toward these hard concrete sidewalks below.

I wondered if that was what Rose was thinking about when she had built her own tiny version of the same building her mother had dove off of. Rose's Lego buildings were like tombstones, I realized.

A plastic cemetery of tiny skyscrapers.

22

aturday evening I hopped up the stairwell steps, trying to get to Vega's apartment as fast as I could. On the way up I almost bumped into Chivonne and Erika, who was walking down.

"Watch out, Lolly!" Chivonne shouted. "You almost knocked us over!"

I said sorry on my way by. Erika was pregnant again, I had noticed, with a big scarf wrapped around her neck. That girl *stayed* with child, like Ma would'a said.

Vega's ma, Mrs. Vega, answered their door. For a minute she just stood there, though, blocking my way and squinting at me. Mrs. Vega was short and round. There was no squeezing past her. After a second, she just exhaled all heavy and stepped aside so I could come into their apartment.

He must'a really been in trouble this time, like his message had said. Vega's ma had never slowed me down before. The Vegas' place was like my second crib.

It was always so neat in Vega's apartment. Especially

compared to our unit on the seventh floor. I mean, me and Jermaine had always kept our room picked up, but our mother was a slob; she hated to clean.

I started to head back toward Vega's room. It was chilly in here, like their heat was broke.

Mrs. Vega shouted something after me in Spanish, but I didn't know what she had said because she had said it so fast.

"*¿Mi amigo está bien?*" I asked her in Spanish.

"No, no!" she shouted back at me. Everything was always shouts up here. "He no leave this *apartamento*, Lolly! *¡Es una lástima!* A shame!" She threw up her hands and rushed into the kitchen.

Inside Vega's bedroom were a bunch of kids, all of them related to him. Three of his teenaged cousins, Luis, Dalvin and Junior, were all huddled near the open window, smoking.

It was freezing in here. When Rose and me were out earlier, it had been nice, but now the sun had gone down.

Nervous, his cousins glanced at me and then smirked.

I knew Vega's mami wouldn't like his cousins smoking in here. She didn't allow no cigarettes in their place. Not even her husband could smoke, which was why he was always hotboxing in the stairwell or down in front of the building.

Vega had told me that when his mother was a little girl in Santiago, her dad had accidentally set their house on fire with a lit cigarette.

Ever since then she had hated smokers.

Even though she later married one.

I was surprised to see Vega's cousin Frito in a chair in the corner talking on his phone. He nodded at me and kept conversatin'. His right arm was in a blue cast. I guess from that bullet that found him.

When I stepped into the room, Vega's young sister, Iris, jumped up from the floor and ran to give me a hug. She had left the bowl of *sancocho* she was devouring on the carpet. Mrs. Vega made the best *sancocho,* with big chunks of pork and lots of plantains. I was eyeing it, hungry.

I picked Iris up like I always did and sat her on my hip. She was heavy. And only six. Too chunky. Her ma fed them too much.

Vega had a older sister, who was at Brooklyn College. She lived in the dorms and was big as a house too.

"Cas is grounded," Iris sadly told me about her brother.

Vega was flicking through stuff on his phone. *"Dímelo, chan,"* he said to me.

"Nothing, man," I answered. "What did you do?"

"He left his new coat somewhere and can't remember," Iris said.

Frito sucked his teeth at this. I sat Iris down on the rug, my back aching. Frito hung up his phone and stood, grimacing. He rubbed his right shoulder.

"They got out the bullet?" I asked him.

Frito nodded. "I was lucky. My doctors say it just missed my blood vessel here."

I exhaled a puff of air.

"Lolly, do us a favor," Frito said, glancing at Vega. "Tell your homie to man up."

"Vete pa' carajo," Vega told him without looking up from his phone.

Frito grinned and whistled at their cousins smoking by the window. "Let's go," he told them. They all slapped hands with me and Vega before disappearing, dragging Iris with them.

I sat down beside Vega.

"I can't believe you lost the coat your grandmother gave you," I said.

He rolled over in his bed and faced the wall.

"I didn't lose it," Vega said to the wall and me. "I gave it to those two dudes."

"Gave it? *What* two dudes?" But I knew before I even finished asking.

Vega told me that Harp and Gully had run up on him this afternoon just like they had run up on me this morning. Only Vega wasn't lucky enough to have Rose bum-rush them. They caught him by himself, coming home from his violin lesson.

I hoped that Rose smashing Harp and Gully wasn't the reason they had jumped Vega. That might'a put those two dudes in a bad mood for the rest of the day. I know it would me.

"They said, 'Tell your cousin Frito to join our set!'" Vega said.

And then Harp and Gully had gave him the same choice they had tried to give me, which really wasn't no choice. They made Vega give them his coat that he had got for Three Kings.

They let him keep his violin.

"I gotta do something, Loll," Vega told me. "Frito says it. Or you know they won't never stop."

"Yeah. What else Frito say?"

Vega didn't speak. Started chewing his bottom lip.

He had lied about this to his mother and father—told them he had lost his coat—because he knew if he'd told them the truth about them boys taking it from him, he would'a got a worse whupping from his parents.

There was something extra evil about the way that Harp and Gully stole stuff. They would make you give them your swag instead of them actually snatching it off you. That way, I thought, if they got caught, they could just tell the cops, "Hey, it was a gift. We ain't no thieves."

But more important, them forcing you to share your belongings, it played with your head. Made you feel less than human. Like you had no power.

Like you needed to find some way to get it back.

In the city room Vega sat on a upside-down pickle bucket playing his violin while he watched me and Rose build. He was still mad. And playing a sad song.

In fact, Vega's music was making me sad even though I had been feeling all right before. It's funny how music can do that to you.

I guess all art is like that. Making art, you can sure change people. Make them feel a certain way or think a certain way.

Mr. Ali had said that what we were doing in the city room was art. I hadn't even thought of it like that before, but I think Ali was right. We were creating worlds in here.

Lately, I had been feeling like it was just something that I had to do.

Like I didn't have no choice in it.

I wanted to do it forever.

"What is that?" I asked Vega.

He paused playing his violin and told me, "Tchaikovsky." And then he went right back to playing it. I sighed.

I glanced over at Rose, who was bent over a model,

building a girder. She didn't seem bothered by Vega's sad music. Rose didn't show her emotions too much. She hid them from everybody.

But when her emotions popped, watch out, man!

Vega set down his violin.

"You playing made me depressed," I told him.

He shrugged. "Music should bring tears to the eyes of women," Vega said. "That's what Beethoven and Ms. D. say. You must be a girl, Lolly."

"You made that up."

"So these new Rose buildings are models of all them buildings you two saw downtown?" Vega asked.

"Uh-huh," I said. "I don't know how she remembers them all. Keeps it up here." I tapped my forehead. "This one here is the Hearst Tower." I showed him some of the pictures I took on my phone.

"Man!" Vega said over Rose's shoulder. "How you do it, Big Rose? Remember everything with all that detail? That's perfect."

Rose stood up straight, stretched her back and turned to us. "I just do it," she said to Vega. "It's easy. They're there already. All over the city." She looked at us like, How do you *not* know this? "Lolly does it too, but his come out of his head. Just his head."

She went back to adding on another story to her miniature Hearst. Vega stooped to get a better look at her

St. Nick buildings. He stayed down on the floor for a minute, squinting.

"This is different, Rosamund," he said, pointing at something there. Rose didn't answer him, but kept working. "These little stars here, Loll. What's she done here?"

I stooped down beside him, not knowing what he was talking about. But then I saw them. Something I'd never seen before. Down beside Rose's St. Nick Houses there were all these little stars.

Shiny.

Golden stickers.

She had stuck golden star stickers on her model where all the sidewalks were. This was new, I thought. I was surprised because every other part of her city was exactly like the real-life buildings. Except these little gold stars.

"Yeah," I said. "What's this, Rose?"

Without looking up from her business, she said, "'Rosamund, when you die, they bury you, but your soul flies to the stars. Your mama, your daddy—they were buried under the ground, but they're stars now, girl, stars beneath our feet.'"

Vega and me stood there, thinking about this. We had buried Jermaine. He was a star now too.

"Sounds like a poem," Vega said to Rose.

"It *is* a poem," Rose said. "In one of Gran's books."

Later on, Vega reminded me, "I told you she was keeping track of the dead bodies."

·+ +·

"So Harmonee was built and designed by the Moneekrom family dynasty. But the evil Swarm has abducted King Blaze. His son, Prince Stellar, fights to rescue his father and drive the Swarm monsters out of Harmonee. Prince Stellar leads a group of heroes called the Star Drivers. The Star Drivers are the good guys and whale on the monsters so bad, the Swarm flees to a totally different galaxy."

"Does Prince Stellar rescue his dad?" Vega asked.

"I haven't decided that yet. It might make a good cliff-hanger," I said.

Vega had been listening to me tell my story. Him and me had just finished circling around the new edges of Harmonee. He took a step back to take in the whole thing, which stretched from one side of the old storage room to the other.

"Yo, this is *chévere*, Lolly," he said. "This whole other world from tiny bricks and your head."

I felt like I had done something.

23

I rolled my bike out of our building's elevator and rode over to meet Daryl R. and Kofi on Eighth Av'. They were waiting for me right on the corner in front of the barbershop like Daryl's message had said.

It felt good to be back on my bike. It was already the middle of March. The weather wasn't so cold like it had been.

Kofi and Daryl had just got fresh cuts at the barber's. This was a different one from Jermaine's, but I'd still never been allowed to go inside. Ma usually shaved my head herself with our electric clippers. She didn't trust any barbershops no more.

All three of us on our bikes, Kofi, Daryl and me went pedaling down to 110th Street and turned left to cruise over toward the East Side, Spanish Harlem. On the right was the top of Central Park and the Harlem Meer, which was a little lake where you could go fishing in the summer.

Mr. Ali had taken us down there last year.

We rode over to Park Av' and turned to head uptown again. This street might'a been one of my fave places in Harlem. I liked it because of the old-timey-looking bridge that ran all along the street, up above you. That bridge was where the trains rolled on.

The rocks and bricks in this bridge felt like they were one of the original things anybody had built in New York City. Like something out of a castle.

We made our way north to 145th, and Daryl stopped at the fish place there to buy a soda and order of fries. While Kofi and me was waiting on him was when I saw Rockit.

Rockit was sitting in his truck, parked along the sidewalk. I could see he was murdering a fried-fish sandwich. On my bike, I scooted over beside the driver's side of his truck where he sat and yelled at him through his window.

"Rockit!" I shouted.

He ducked and started to reach for something. When he saw it was me, he grinned and rolled down his window.

"Little man," he said. "Don't be rolling up on me like that. Something might happen."

"What you doing?" I asked.

"Eating fish," he said. "You want one? It's good."

I shook my head. I noticed the right side of Rockit's face was all swole and his eye was red, like he had got pistol-whipped by somebody. He wasn't as unperturbed as he usually was.

"I never heard from you about that Christmas present," Rockit said. "I guess your moms took it from you."

"Nah," I said. "Thanks, man. She let me keep it. Me and Vega play it all the time. Thanks, Rock."

He nodded all slow. Rockit seemed like he needed some rest, like he hadn't slept in, well, *forever.*

"Yo, like I told you, that's from 'Maine. Your brother wanted that for you. The night they got him, he told me he had been planning to get that for you, that particular brand. He said he had always wanted a game system when he was little, but your parents never had the paper."

I nodded. I was in the street talking to him. A car drove by kind of close to me. I picked up my bike between my legs and scooted it closer to his truck.

"Jermaine had big plans for you, Lolly," Rockit went on.

Hearing Rockit say that made me tense up.

"You need help with anything, little man?" he asked. "Ain't nobody bothering you? You need a job?"

I shook my head.

"'Cuz if some niggas was bothering you," Rockit said, "just let me know and I'll get involved. Stomp that out real quick."

I could feel my blood rush to my face. Though it was chilly outside, I was getting hot. I was about to tell him about Harp and Gully and me and Vega. Rockit probably would handle it. He could make them hurt. He could . . .

"Yeah," Rockit went on, "'Maine wanted more for you. If he had lived, I know he was gonna make sure you got some kinda college."

I froze. Suddenly wanted to smash Rockit in his big, dumb face. "He never talked about all that to me" was all I said.

"There was a lotta stuff he never talked about with you." He stared down at his fish, frowned and tossed it into the street. "Look. Give a brother a call sometime," he said. "Send me a shout-out. Something. I'm gonna hook you up, Loll. Like 'Maine would'a wanted. You remind me of him. Look just like 'im. You need any money?"

I shook my head.

"A'ight, then," he said, all drowsy. "Call me sometime."

I nodded, but I didn't think I would. "I gotta go."

"I gotta bounce too," Rockit said, starting up his engine. "I'm tired, man. Just . . . *tired.* . . . I'll see you, little man."

He drove off. Daryl, Kofi and me pedaled up the steep hill on 145th Street, headed back to the West Side. I knew all that pumping would help pedal off all this anger I suddenly felt.

That hill was always a monster, but we glided down the other side.

Flying fast like this, down big, long Sugar Hill, really made me feel free. Like I was about to take off.

Kofi and Daryl, on either side of me, were smiling.

On our right side, suddenly everything had turned brown and green. St. Nicholas Park came up. We whizzed by the park, glancing toward the branches every now and then.

Finally, near the bottom of Sugar Hill, Daryl braked.

He pedaled over to the edge of the park. Kofi and me rolled our bikes up behind him.

I didn't know why he'd stopped. If he hadn't, we could'a rolled all the way down to St. Nick Houses just on momentum. After a minute, I realized what Daryl was doing.

I searched too, but I couldn't see our coyote nowhere. I had packed my tablet. Just in case I wanted to sketch it. For a second, I thought something rustling the grass might'a been him, but it was just a little black squirrel.

Daryl reached into his backpack and placed the French fries he had just bought onto a park bench. He scrutinized the trees one more time and then we all biked off.

As I pedaled, I kept peering into the park for any signs, but didn't see none.

Afterward Kofi had told me that Daryl had been leaving fries for that coyote ever since we saw it.

Our coyote was part of a species in danger. Hunted down and shot up.

We knew how it felt.

24

Sunnshyne stuck her African scarf–wearing head inside our city room to see what was up. At least, that's what she had said. To me, it seemed like she had just wanted to instigate something negative.

Like always.

Her and Vega were arguing.

Like always.

Only this time they had been arguing about my artwork.

Ever since I had started hanging out with Rose, Sunny had gotten more and more despicable about what I was doing. I remembered back when I had commenced my city, she had thought it was supreme.

But now...

"Well, I think it's just *childish*," Sunny went on. "I mean, Wallace is too old for all this Lego junk."

"What you talking about, Moonshyne?" Vega asked her. "Twelve's not too old. What is childish is running around

St. Nick acting like you run a detective agency. That's as childish as dirty diapers."

"*Shut up.* I'm telling you," she said, "it's sweet that they put all this work into these Legos... but for what?"

"It's *artistic*," he said.

"Toys ain't art."

"Have you heard the whole story Loll came up with? For Harmonee?"

"That's nonsense."

"Don't call it that, Sunny!"

"I'm saying, think of all their extra studies they been missing out on. It's a waste." Sunny shook her head. "The only thing more wasteful is Big Head over there, *regurgitating* the PJs."

"That means puking," Vega said.

Sunnshyne was impressed. "*Anyway,* at least Lolly's shows more imagination than his future baby mama."

She pointed her finger at Rose in the corner.

Rose, who had been sitting, legs crossed, leaped to her feet. Before me or Vega could say or do anything, she was standing over Sunny with her fist raised above her head. She was about to deck her.

I held my breath and locked my eyes tight. I had seen Rose in action. After a minute, I hadn't heard Sunny's bones break, so I peeked.

Rose was still standing there over Sunny. Instead of

clubbing her, though, Rose lowered her fist all slow and glared at her. She told Sunny, "When you die, they bury you."

"What?" Sunny said.

Rose let a grin flash over her face and folded her hands over her chest. "You're ugly," Rose told Sunny. "You act ugly."

Sunny glared at Rose like she didn't know who Rose was. Then Sunny breathed out a heavy puff of air and her face seemed to melt, get all soft. She left the city room, looking worried, rushing right past Mr. Ali, who had been standing in the doorway this whole time.

I wasn't sure if Rose had seen him there or not. I didn't think she had.

"Making progress, Rosamund!" Ali yelled across the room. "Use your words instead of your fists." He strolled into the room with his hands folded behind his back. "Rose! Lolly! Come here for a sec," Ali shouted. "Casimiro, let us alone. I need to speak with your conspirators here."

Vega left the room. Before he did, he gave me a look that said *Game over.* By the frown cut into Mr. Ali's face, it did seem like we were in trouble for something.

He gathered me and Rose in the center of the city room and stared at us for a few seconds before opening his mouth again.

"I got some terrible news," Ali started.

I had figured that. We'd been having our office chats less and less lately. I started to believe Ali was going to say we needed to have more of them again. Like I wasn't making progress like he had wanted.

But I *had* been. . . .

Ali said this: "I'm very proud of all you two've done over the past few months. You should be proud of yourselves—we *all* are in the center."

He paused. A sad smile crept across his expression.

"A new fitness program is moving in," Ali went on. "You're gonna have to tear down your cities to make room for it."

What?

"They'll be using this room for health ed," he said. "I'm sorry. This is an awful lot of work, but I guess you knew it couldn't stay up here forever."

Rose didn't react at all. My mouth hung open.

"Rose, I am particularly proud of you with all of the progress you've made. You've really blossomed. . . ."

Without a word, Rose ran straight at her Lego city and began tearing it apart.

"Rosamund!" Ali yelled. "You can wait, girl. They don't have to come down this minute. I'll let you know."

Across the room, Rose stopped and began rebuilding. Mr. Ali rolled his eyes. He turned back to me and started talking again.

I stood there and watched Mr. Ali's mouth move. He was talking, but I wasn't hearing.

I hid in my bedroom for most of Saturday.

Vega had been messaging me every few minutes, but I had been ignoring him. I had turned down the volume on my phone because I hadn't wanted to talk to nobody.

I really felt like I didn't have nothing to say. All those days I spent planning, building, dreaming up ideas...

That city *is* me. It will be erased. Everybody in after-school said they loved Harmonee, but they didn't really.

What was the point in doing anything if it was all gonna be destroyed anyhow?

The messed-up thing was that just when I felt like I had been getting all right with Jermaine being gone, him being dead, all this *hostility* had to happen.

I sunk my head into my pillow and just cried.

I figured I would wind up as bad as my rotten city.

In the dark and middle of the night, I stumbled into Ma's bedroom and crawled into her bed next to her. Her paperback of *A Coffin for Dimitrios* was jabbing me, so I set it on her nightstand.

Ma kind of half woke up and grunted. I laid my head on her side and she reached over to hug me against her. She rubbed my head.

I suddenly felt safe. I could feel myself getting drowsy already.

I drifted off, thinking about me and my mother's old story challenges and wishing we could play another one.

I had been avoiding Mr. Ali the past few days, feeling like he had betrayed me. I guess I realized that he really hadn't, but I couldn't help feeling that way for a while.

Tricked.

He finally managed to drag me into his office.

"Mr. Rachpaul, we hardly talk anymore!" Mr. Ali said.

"I know," I said.

"That's a good thing. It means you've improved. All the work you've done up till now I don't want us to lose. I don't want that. I know you don't."

I really didn't care anymore.

He had said he was worried that us having to tear down Harmonee might affect me in a bad way. Might cause me to "backslide." I wondered if he really knew what he was talking about.

I felt I was already starting to go back to how I was.

I was scared to ask him how much longer we had before Harmonee came down.

That day he had pulled out a new sketchbook and handed it to me. His feeling was that I could start drawing my ideas and cities since I wouldn't have the space anymore to build them in real life.

Drawing cities?

I sucked my teeth.

I had been wondering about Rose and how she was going to react to everything we had created getting demolished. I asked Mr. Ali if he was having these convos with Rose, like he had been having with me. He said no, that he wasn't really trained on that level.

"Big Rose is a whole nother bag of groceries," Ali told me, raising his eyebrows.

25

Rose's grandmother finally managed to unlock their front door after spending five minutes fumbling with the locks. She cracked the door and I spotted her face, round and yellow, with rounder eyeglasses that made her eyeballs look bulging.

"I got it!" Gran said with a wheezy smile. "These locks are rusty. Come inside, Mr. Lolly. Rose is almost ready. I'm Dr. Betty Green."

Dr. Betty was old.

She was really heavy and moved around her place really slow, hunched over a plain black cane made of wood. Though Gran's face and my face were at the same height, if she had stood up straight, she would'a been way taller than me.

Inside, their apartment was full of books. Magazines and old newspapers were stacked in heaps everywhere. There were so many piles, you had to wriggle through their apartment in little pathways between the clutter, like you were stumbling through a tight maze.

It smelled funny in here.

A big wooden table sat in the middle of their living room. There were a few books and notebooks on it. I guessed that was where old Gran homeschooled Rose. I also saw a pack of those gold star stickers Rose had stuck on her buildings.

"Have a seat," Gran said. "Would you like some lemonade?"

"No, ma'am," I said. I gazed around at all of the books lining their walls' bookshelves. There were a few framed diplomas on the walls too. They looked like Rose's grandmother had earned them a long time ago.

I sneezed.

"You're admiring my collection," Gran said. "We're partial to poetry here. *Nothing* after the nineteenth century. The greatest poets worked then. I got something for you."

Wheezing, she shuffled over to a bookcase and handed me one of the old, dusty books. It was a small one, like the kind Rose always read during after-school.

"Ms. Phillis Wheatley," Gran said, grinning. "One of our most illustrious Black poets! There is no true poetry any longer. No Blake, Keats, Pope. . . ."

I didn't know what she was talking about. The cover of the poetry book read *The Collected Works of Phillis Wheatley.*

"You may have it," Gran told me.

Poetry?

I knew that I would never, ever read this book.

"Thanks," I said.

Just then, I heard a toilet flush and Rose stepped into the living room, tugging on her hair.

Rose and me caught the subway to Rock Center. I had decided to try to sketch some of the buildings there like Mr. Ali had recommended.

We hadn't talked at all about what Mr. Ali had said the other week, about us having to destroy all our work. He hadn't said when he was expecting us to start deconstruction.

I think both me and Rose were hoping that if we didn't bring it up, then it wouldn't happen. That didn't make any sense, I know. It probably made as much sense as us thinking that our cities would'a stayed there forever.

Rockefeller Center was filled with busy people.

Both Rose and me had been to this part of Midtown before. She said her gran had brought her here for the Christmas tree lighting once. My parents had been taking me here to Tuttle's Toy Emporium since I was little.

Coming to Tuttle's was like visiting someplace magic.

Like the rest of the buildings at Rock Center, Tuttle's had a kind of boring tan Art Deco facade. But on the inside? On the inside there was so much color and so many different kinds of toys that if you tried to pack it all into one first glance, your head would explode.

As soon as you blew through the entrance of Tuttle's, there were two people dressed in giant teddy bear costumes holding the doors open for you. Inside was a room with tall, tall ceilings, three stories high. Escalators took you up to the other toy levels. But in this first, large room there was all kinds of cool stuff to see.

My favorites were the Legos, of course.

They had life-size Lego statues of George Washington, Batman and a Black pirate with a green bird on his shoulder. Of course, my favorite Lego creation in the main room was that enormous green-and-gold dragon that stood twenty feet tall against the back wall.

Dopeness.

In the Lego department on the ground floor there was a gigantic plastic tube filled with blocks. This tube ran all the way up to the second-story balcony, where the people that worked there would keep filling it up with loose Legos, all shapes, sizes and colors. At the bottom of this tube, kids could scoop out blocks and pay for them by the pound like you would grapes or nuts. I guessed that this was where all of my leftover bricks was coming from.

Across from that, there was a funny man in a booth doing magic tricks with cards for the kids. He pulled a bunch of playing cards from out of Rose's sleeve. She was stunned stupid.

Later on, Rose fell in love with a white horse with silver wings. It was a big doll that was large enough for two people to ride on its back.

Then this man on stilts and dressed like a giraffe stole my African hat. He swooped it right off my head and ran away with it. Yelling, I had to chase after him until he gave it back to me. I could tell he hadn't expected me to get as mad as I had.

I watched him glide off with swooshing steps to the other side of the room to bother some other kids.

"Why didn't you help me, Rose!" I said, glaring at her.

Rose glanced at the floor like she had got extra shy all of a sudden.

She got on my nerves sometimes.

One of the people who worked at Tuttle's was able to find Yvonne and lead her to me and Rose. Yvonne was surprised to see me there, where she worked. It was interesting to be in the same place as where all of our Legos were coming from.

Yvonne took a work break and led us outside to the plaza in the middle of Rock Center. We sat outside and talked for a minute, but Yvonne kept twitching around, like she was anxious to get back to work.

She gave me a hug and told me to stop looking so mean. I didn't care.

Me and Rose wandered around Midtown for a while. Rose was quiet. I tried sketching some of the buildings there.

We paused on East 53rd Street, where a new building was being built. Well, actually, they were adding on more floors to the top of an older building.

I made a quick sketch of the construction, all these tiny people up there crawling around the girders like ants on a big tree. Rose seemed to be looking at them too, but not really looking at them.

Afterward we caught the D train up to 1-2-5 and back home to St. Nick. On the subway, I read one of the poems in that book Rose's gran had given me. It was different from what I thought it would be.

Not as dumb.

I read the poem again.

And then began another one.

Imagination! who can sing thy force?
Or who describe the swiftness of thy course?

I started to feel like they were talking to me.

26

I t was dusky outside, but people were out. The Harlem
streets were full. Kids and adults, hanging, enjoying the
nice weather.

Vega and me walked under a tree that was so fragrant-
oozing. I guessed its pink flowers had blossomed and formed
the smell. Like a female's strong perfume.

Soothing.

It reminded me of something in one of those Phillis
Wheatley poems I'd read. And in the distance, I could hear
motorcycle engines roaring just like in a Tupac Shakur video
I had seen online.

As we walked east on the sidewalk, I turned to Vega beside me. Though it was dark, the street lampposts made a
lot of light. Vega shoved his hands in his pockets, his face
turned down toward the ground.

As horrible as I was feeling about having to destroy Harmonee, it relieved me for a minute, just seeing him there.

"Ali tell you when he wants your stuff down?" Vega asked, like he was reading my mind.

He was a true friend, I realized.

"Nah," I said. "I bet it's soon, though. I think that new corny health program is starting up."

"That's messed up, them making you demolish everything," Vega said. "I think it must be hard to be a real artist."

"What you mean?"

"Well, if we was different, you know, been born with money. . . . It's just. . . making good art and music ain't really expected of us. That type of work is unexpected."

"Yeah," I said. "It wasn't meant for us. But I still think you'll be a good violinist. You are now!"

It smelled like rain. I turned up toward the sky and could see heavy clouds.

"Lolly, I think you'll be a good architect. Or whatever you wanna do."

"Thanks, Vega. We both know I won't ever be nothing."

We crossed over Fifth Av' and headed downtown.

In Manhattan, where we lived, Fifth Av' was the divider between the West Side and the East Side. Now, on the East Side, we passed in front of a busy bodega. There was a crowd of kids out front, laughing and dancing to a boom box.

On the next block, a cop car slowed down and eyed us. A white cop dude and his Black female partner shined a light on us, but kept on rolling. Like they was looking for somebody.

Their light burned my eyes. I was glad they didn't bother us. If they had, I might'a done something crazy because of how I was feeling now.

We kept on.

Vega's mami had sent him out to get some rice and green plantains. But she didn't have no money right then to pay for the food, so we were walking to Manny's far-off bodega that would let her have groceries now, but pay for them later.

"Look!" Vega shouted.

Coming up the sidewalk toward us were Sunny and April E. Those girls saw us, but shot right past, ignoring us.

They looked embarrassed and were stepping as fast as they could back toward St. Nick. The crazy thing was April was tugging a small animal on a leash behind her. The leash was attached to a tiny harness snapped around the body of a chicken.

A skinny white chicken.

On a leash.

Vega stared at me wide-eyed. I couldn't believe it either. He yelled after them, "How's that detective biz, girls!"

"EDK Investigators and chicken walkers!" I shouted.

I could see Sunny's shoulders shrink. Vega laughed

until he cried. Finally, we continued toward Manny's bodega.

"That was *surreal*," I said. "Walking a chicken."

"What's that word mean?" Vega asked. "Surreal?"

"I don't know exactly, *manin*, but I think we just saw it."

There was about a dozen people hanging out in front of the store by the time we got there. One of them was wild Darrell B. from after-school and his friend Dulé from Senegal. Dulé was a giant.

We slapped hands.

Inside the cramped bodega, I took my time searching for a snack that would satisfy how I felt. In the end, I decided to grab a big bag of Utz Red Hot chips and handed Manny, the owner, four quarters. Manny put the chips in a black plastic bag and handed it to me.

"I'll wait on you out front," I told Vega. He was still fumbling through the plantains, trying to find one that wasn't too ripe.

Outside in front of the bodega, everybody had left. It had started to shower and people had scattered like cockroaches do when you switch on a light. I heard a motorcycle engine moaning far off.

I was ready to head back to St. Nick.

Little drops of rain was sprinkling from the atmosphere. I sighed and turned my face up toward the sky, letting my forehead get sprinkled. It tickled.

I closed my eyes and wondered how far these drip-drops of water had fallen just to wind up on my face. The word "facade" popped into my head for some reason. I had just learned about it in that book.

"This how you *St. Niggas* take showers?" somebody said. I opened my eyes and right off got jerked up into the air and slammed down hard onto the sidewalk.

From down on the ground, I frowned up at Harp and Gully, standing over me. Gully was bent over, his face sneering into mine. Harp was standing behind him, hooting.

"This the *East* Side," Gully said. "Your big-head gorilla ain't here to protect you."

Just then, the door to the bodega flung open. They both glanced over at Vega. He was standing there with his mouth open, holding a black plastic bag in one hand and his phone in the other.

Harp stepped to him and snatched them both.

"Oh!" Vega shouted. He swung at Harp, who dodged and sent his fist flying against Vega's dome. Vega fell back against the door.

"Get *his*," Harp ordered Gully, who tried to grope into my pockets.

Lying on my back, I stuck Gully in his jaw, but he acted

like he scarcely felt it. I kept whaling punches. He blocked some, then clocked me upside my head. The back of my skull bounced off the sidewalk's rocky concrete.

Everything switched fuzzy.

I could hear Vega holler and struggle with Harp.

I kept trying to smack Gully, who had straddled me, but everything I did was in slow motion; my fists dragged through water. I felt his hands jam into my jean pockets again.

Gully emptied everything onto the ground, jerking my pockets inside out before he found my phone. I managed to crack him one last time on his chin before he stood up and kicked me.

"Cool! You gave us your phone anyway, Lollypop!" Gully said. "Good looking out!" He made a popping sound with his lips.

I heard Harp tell Vega, "As long as Frito keeps holding out, this is what you get! Tell your cuz!"

Then Manny the bodega owner yelled, "Hey! Hey! You boys! *Lárguense! Lárguense!* Oooh!"

And next I heard footsteps sprint off. I sat up in time to see the backs of Harp and Gully making it down the block. Manny stood on the sidewalk with a wooden baseball bat, waving it after them.

Vega was sitting on the ground too, his back propped against the shop. His nose was bloody.

I felt my jeans, but I knew already that I wouldn't find nothing. I knew that those punks had robbed me. My keys and pocket change were scattered across the sidewalk with Vega's blood.

It started to rain harder.

I sat there on the wet ground watching Harp and Gully turn the corner. I pounded the concrete with my fist until I broke skin.

· ✚ ✚ ✚ ·

Cold as iced-over pavement.

That's how I felt in the back of the police car. It was those same two cops—the white dude and Black woman that had shined their light on us—who showed up at the bodega after Manny had called them.

They asked Vega and me lots of questions, but me and him didn't answer most of them. We didn't know who had jumped us or why. We didn't get a good look at them. We didn't want no ride back to where we lived.

That was the last thing Vega and me had wanted—to get dropped off at St. Nick projects by two cops and have everybody see us and start wondering if we had snitched on somebody.

The only reason we were riding in the back of the cop car now was that Manny knew Vega's ma and had made the police take us home. So we wouldn't get jumped again. He even gave them the address.

Now here we were.

My head burned like it was full of Red Hot chips. It felt swole too. Ma wouldn't like that. Vega looked worse.

When you ride in the back of a cop car, does that mean you're arrested?

They were in the front and we were caught in the back. I felt like a crook, like I had done something wrong. This was our first time here. I wondered if we'd ever be riding in the backseat again.

I didn't like it.

It was still raining. It had gotten harder. Nobody was saying nothing. Except for the squeak of the windshield wipers and the squawking police radios, all you could hear was the rain hitting the car roof.

We stopped at a red light at Frederick Douglass Boulevard and 125th and I glanced over at Vega. He was scrunched over on the other side of the seat, leaning against the window, looking out at the rain.

It was dark, but the red light from the stop signal lit up his face like a fire.

"You gonna tell your cousin?" I whispered.

Vega turned to me slow, tilting his head onto his shoulder. One of his eyes was swole. He almost looked like he was about to go to sleep. His eyes, though, the way they looked at me, his eyes weren't sleepy.

They were hard. And something else.

He had changed.

The old Vega had been left behind on that sidewalk in front of Manny's bodega. This new Vega in the back of the cop car with me, he was somebody I hadn't met yet.

27

The tiniest ones made up my brother's face.

It was all Legos. Tiny brown-skinned Legos.

And I remembered for the first time in a long time that scar Jermaine had. That tiny scar on his cheek he had got from tripping into the chain-link fence on the playground when he was a kid.

Years later, I asked Jermaine how exactly he had got that scar and he told me he had been in a fight with another playground kid and got shoved. One of the pieces of the metal fence had caught him.

The scar on his cheek, you could hardly see, but it had stayed with him.

His face was huge now. Built all out of Legos just like the Black pirate statue at Tuttle's. But now Jermaine's face was glowing too, the blocks turning from brown to glowing red and then growing out of a brick wall, like flowers budding in fast motion.

His face was stuck into a red-brick wall.

It was the wall outside Manny's.

Jermaine's rectangle block eyes stared at me from out of the bricks and I realized that this was crazy and that was also when my own eyes opened.

The ceiling.

I was lying flat on my back in my own bedroom.

For a minute, I felt like I couldn't move. But when I finally did move, I suddenly wished I hadn't. My whole body was stiff and sore. It took me a minute to remember why.

I remembered what happened last night in front of the bodega.

Jermaine's face like a red-brick wall.

I reached up to feel my own face. The corners of my eyes were wet. I closed them again.

Tight.

My bones were still aching when I snuck into the kitchen for breakfast. Ma was already in there, making her special Lipton and lemon tea. She was wearing her security-guard uniform, about to head off to work at the courts.

I slid down behind the table and started in on the bowl of cornflakes she had waiting for me. Everything was going okay until she turned around from the stove and asked why I was wearing my African hat at her table.

I had it pulled down low over my forehead.

The night before, I had been lucky. Vega and me asked the two cops that had picked us up at Manny's to drop us off near 130th and Seventh Av', so we could walk across the street to our building.

That way, we avoided any attention from being seen socializing with cops. That was Vega's smart idea.

And I was more lucky that Ma was back in her room when I came in, and I went straight to my own room. She didn't see me last night and I was hoping that she wouldn't get a good look at me this morning.

Boy, I was wrong.

"Jumped!" she yelled. "What you mean you got jumped?"

Ma ripped my hat off my head and covered her mouth when she saw my huge bump. She turned my head from side to side, I guess checking out the rest of my damage.

She stood staring at me for a minute, hand still covering her mouth.

"Wallace, are you okay?"

"I feel fine, Ma," I lied. "Believe me."

"Who did this?"

I shrugged. It even hurt to do that. "Some dudes. We don't know who. Outside a bodega on the East Side."

"You don't know?" Ma asked. "You did not see them?"

"It was dark and rainy," I said, stirring my cornflakes. I let my eyeballs fall to the floor.

"Why wasn't I told about this?" she asked. "You said the

police dropped you off last night? They should have said something!"

"They did what we asked," I said. "We didn't want no excitement—"

Ma hissed.

I never heard her straight-up hiss before. This was new. My mother was a snake now.

"What did I tell you about that phone?" she yelled. "Huh? What did I tell you!"

"You blaming me?"

"It's all your fault!"

"Huh? *My* fault?"

"Yes!" she said. "First you bug me to get you that damn phone and then you let yourself get jumped, flashing it about!"

I didn't like that. "I wasn't flashing it," I said.

Ma shook her finger in my face. "I warned you. I warned you. And now look at you, beaten and bruises." She spun around, paced toward the window.

With her back turned, I decided to snap my hat back on my head. My arms burned to lift them. My feelings on the inside were beginning to feel hurt too.

"You could'a been killed," I heard her say, all low. Looking tired, she turned back around to me. "Finish up and get showered, okay? We're going to the clinic."

"The *health* clinic?"

"No!" Ma barked. "The *animal* clinic, fool. What you think?"

"But you got work," I said. "You're late."

Ma exhaled. "Not today. Now hurry up, Lolly. Get ready. You know how long they make you wait down there."

I stood up to head to the bathroom. I had only ate a little bit, but I wasn't really hungry anymore. I turned to leave.

"You shouldn't blame me," I said.

She answered with the biggest sigh.

That Monday at after-school Rose and me worked in quiet.

And side by side, sometimes us crisscrossing bodies when we had to lean across one another to stick a Lego into place.

I didn't bother telling her about me getting jumped. For a minute, I was afraid that she might get hurt herself, going out to seek revenge for me. But by the way she looked at me in our city room, it seemed like she had already known.

She looked at me kinda sorry.

Either way, I don't know why I had been worried that Rose might get hurt going after Harp and Gully—she had already beat the two of them dudes, practically by herself.

But me and Vega couldn't do nothing against them.

Ma always said not to underestimate a woman.

I decided to take a break from building. I took a step back from our latest creation to get a good look at it.

This new thing was different. We'd never built anything exactly like this before. I was proud. And sad too.

"What's that?" Vega asked.

I turned and watched him shuffle into the city room. His swole eye looked a lot better.

"Where was you?" I asked him. "You missed most of the day."

Vega kept walking over to what we were building. Rose stopped for a moment to stare at Vega's eye. He watched her do this and frowned.

"Still on punishment?" I asked Vega. He didn't say nothing, but walked around to the other side of our new project. He squinted at something on the other side.

"This is crooked" was all he said.

I scrunched my face. I told him, "It's a bridge, man. We know it's crooked, Vega. We're going to swap in some *other* bricks on that side later. Ones from . . ."

Vega had stooped down to make an adjustment that nobody had asked him to make. He tried to push up one of the brick walls on our bridge and wound up collapsing the whole side.

Rose and me stared at him like he was crazy.

But instead of apologizing, Vega kinda smirked and then

just shook his head and started walking backward toward the door. He had a mean half smile on his face.

I was pissed.

Pointing at Vega, I started after him, but got jerked back. Rose had reached out and grabbed my shoulder. I grimaced.

"Rose!" I said. "Are you crazy?" My back was still sore, on fire.

She just glared at me, then walked to the other side of our bridge, where Vega had done his damage, and she started to rebuild.

It took me a while to help.

It took even longer for me to cool off. I had been feeling irritated lately, but Vega had really tried it with me.

Like he sunk me lower.

28

I crouched down some more to get a closer peek inside one of our girder grids. The columns were okay, but I still thought we could'a made a simpler foundation. We had wasted too many blocks.

But, I remembered, none of that really mattered anymore. For the past week, Rose and me had been working on this last Lego piece together.

We'd run out of time.

In a few minutes, they would come in here to move our bridge out of the city room and into the courtyard. The two big doors that opened to the outside were standing wide open, and every now and then, I could hear beats booming from the DJ setting up out there.

"Lolly, you ready to move this stuff to the court?" Mr. Ali asked.

He had entered the city room through the double doors. Sparkling sunlight jetted from behind him, leaving his face in the dark.

The black shape of Rose's husky body wandered in through the doors. She waited beside Ali, rubbing one of her elbows.

"When you die, they bury you," I heard Rose say. "But your soul flies to the stars."

I stood up and frowned; my back was still a little sore from Gully slamming me to the concrete last week. The doctor at the clinic thought I'd be fine. Ma and Daddy were relieved to hear there was no real damage.

I thought about how Vega and me had told our parents that we had got curb-stomped in front of the bodega and that some random thieves had snatched our phones. I guess it was okay that we'd lied and told them that we didn't know who had jumped us.

I was afraid of somebody calling me a snitch.

My lump above my right eye still stung a little. And my butt stung from falling on the concrete. I hadn't told anybody that part, though.

For almost the whole week, every time I moved, I hurt. It was like a little reminder of getting beat down a zillion times a day.

I couldn't forget it.

What might'a hurt the most was the fact that all the photos that I had taken on Rose and me's architecture tours were gone.

I hadn't even backed them up.

"I guess I'm ready," I finally answered back to Mr. Ali. "Might as well get this done."

Standing outside this morning in the courtyard between the buildings at St. Nick, I shoved half of a hot dog in my mouth.

The DJ started playing the clean version of one of my favorite songs. It didn't sound as real with all the cursing taken out. At these types of center events, Mr. Ali wouldn't let anybody play any music that he said had a harmful message, or grimy lyrics.

Ma couldn't come because she was making up that day she missed work.

I wondered where stupid Vega was. I hadn't seen him since he pulled apart our Legos days ago.

I kept thinking that I should message him, but then remembered that my phone got boosted. And so had his. Remembering this pissed me off. It was funny how in just a couple of months I had got so used to doing everything on my phone.

I peeped a few of the people that had showed up so far to the health fair and cookout. I held a cold can of soda to my head to numb my forehead.

It felt good. It had become a habit.

"Nah! Lolly!" little Jasmine David yelled. She ducked

and spun and dodged around me in a circle. I gulped the last of my dog. "I bet you can't catch me!" she went on.

I leaped toward her and plucked one of her braids. She screamed and sped off, grinning. She was only seven.

I chased after a lot of the youngsters in the courtyard, their parents watching from the ring of park benches that circled it. Mr. Ali called for me to come over to the middle, where the DJ was set up and where parts of our cities had been moved.

"Lolly," Ali said. He crinkled his face at me. "Where's Rose? You two should stand closer to your creations. In case somebody wants to ask."

I frowned at him. "What are they gonna ask?"

"Questions!" he said. "Just stay close, brother. And go find Rose."

How was I supposed to do both at the same time?

Ali started talking to the DJ about something.

Two sections of my city and two sections of Rose's had been moved outside this morning. It was odd to see them out here shining in the sunlight instead of under the dim lights of the storage room. Being on show like this, outside in the middle of the hood, made Harmonee even more like a fantasy city, all bright and bizarre.

Mr. Ali's idea to do this had been a legitimate idea, though at first I hadn't been too sure. Rose and me had collaborated on something fresh, just for today. We had built a oversize Lego bridge that connected one of her city sections to one of mines.

On Rose's side of the bridge, the design was pretty everyday—just like her city was like real life. But toward the middle of our bridge, the layout started to change. It kind of blended more into my own fantasy style so that by the time the structure reached my city section, it was made up of everything straight out of my head and all dream-kissed.

It was kind of *hot*, really.

And the bridge sat up high enough in the air that little kids or short people could actually bow under it, if they wanted.

Building the new bridge had kinda helped me not think so much about what had happened with Harp and Gully. Vega needed something like that—so he wouldn't think on it too much.

I guess playing his violin was like that, but I had barely seen Vega at all. He had stopped coming to after-school. He should'a been here today.

I took in the people in the courtyard. It was more full than before. I didn't see Rose anywhere. She was probably still sulking too.

I felt deserted.

I bobbed my head and looked over at the Madtown section of Harmonee that we had moved out here. Madtown was where all the monsters lived.

A lady and her little boy had walked up to it. Her son,

about four, kept trying to touch my buildings, but the woman kept jerking him back.

The mother smiled at me. She had some long fake eyelashes. "You Lolly, right?" she asked.

"Yeah," I said.

"You and Big Rose are the straight-up *artistes*!" she said. "We met before. Years ago, over at Janine's. You were about his age, basically." She pointed to her boy. "I'm Sadie."

"Nice to meet you. Or *remeet* you."

"You and Rose need to be very, very proud of this," Sadie said.

I grinned.

· ✛ ✛ ✛ ·

"Say cheese!"

I beamed again and this ancient dude snapped a pic with his phone.

"There we go," he said, viewing how the photo turned out. "The master architect! Thanks for the picture, brother."

"Thank *you*," I said.

He and his old wife cheesed at me one more time and wandered over to a purple health-department booth where the staff were taking people's blood pressure.

The whole afternoon had been like that. All these people I didn't know, and a lot of people I did know, had rushed up to me and told me how much they loved my art.

I hadn't seen Rose since we'd moved the Legos this morning. It was almost four o'clock now. And Vega hadn't showed up yet either. I really didn't want him to miss this.

I guess he was mad at me.

Even Freddy's friend, that boy Butteray Jones, had showed.

He was a weird sort of kid. Really dressed all-out with a country way of talking and a old-style hat made out of purple plaid. Butteray said he didn't stay in the PJs, but him and his parents stayed up on Sugar Hill.

This was my first time meeting him.

He liked my African hat and called it "cute." He must'a been gay, I thought. Straight boys didn't call nothing cute unless they were talking about a female.

"So you're Lolly," he said, looking me up and down. He was staring at me now, like I was some character out of a book he had read and I had come to life.

"Freddy told you about me?" I asked.

Butteray shook his head back and forth real quick. "Naw," he said in that funny Southern way. "Freddy and me don't barely speak. I'm cool with his brother."

"Oh, cool." We stood like that for a while. I was about to say something, but he spoke next.

"I been the one giving your girl lessons," he said.

I was lost.

Butteray grinned. He had this big gap between his two front teeth. He looked like a idiot.

"Your girl Sunnshyne?" Butteray said. "My folks own Aunt Cushie's Southern Café on the Hill. I been the one teaching Sunny how to cook. Chocolate-covered candies at first, then other stuff... jalapeños..."

I was just starting to ask myself in my head if this kid might be *super* weird, but then he ran off all of a sudden and he answered my question for me.

Butteray Jones.

Nuts.

Just then, Sunnshyne and her mother showed, strolling up from behind me. Butteray must'a spotted them coming before I had. They were hard to miss. Sunny and her moms were both wearing matching African head wraps.

Super ultra colors.

Her mother, Tootsie, was a Black militant and a waitress. Tootsie was wearing a black T-shirt that read: NEW BLACK PANTHER PARTY.

After that, I noticed that Sunny's arm was in a sling. When I saw her like that, I suddenly felt sorry for her, even kind of worried.

"You okay?" I asked Sunny, pointing at her sling.

She nodded. "Who was that?" Sunny asked me. "Was that Butteray?"

I nodded. "I guess."

Sunny's moms asked her, "Butteray from the café?"

How many Butterays could there be in Harlem? In the world, even?

"*Hmph!*" Tootsie went. "I wonder why he didn't say hi? I hope I'm not in trouble at work. . . ."

Sunny looked kind of funny and then told me, "Congratulations, Lolly. Everybody loves what you made. I was wrong."

Tootsie bulged her eyes. "Wait a minute, Sunny. My hearing must be acting up, 'cuz I thought I just heard you say you were *wrong* about something? But I *know* I must'a misheard!"

Sunnshyne ignored her. "Lolly, your city, Harmonee, is beautiful. You *are* a real artist."

I felt warm. My bump had started to itch, so I tilted my African hat away from it. Sunny's mother could see the bruise above my eye for the first time and her eyes popped. She took a step toward me.

"What happened to your face?" Tootsie asked, looking alarmed.

I shrugged. "Nothing."

Sunny's mother squinted her eyes at me.

"Your bump is smaller," Sunny told me.

"Oh, yeah." I looked away and used my hat to cover my bruise again.

"Well, uh, you should be truly proud, baby," her moms said to me, smacking on some gum.

When I asked Sunny how she hurt her arm, she

suddenly looked humiliated. Her mother kissed her on her forehead and put an arm around her and said only, "A wild-wolf chase."

"What?" I asked her ma.

"Never mind, Lolly," Sunny said. "And I told you, Mama: it's not a *wolf.*"

Anyway, I was thankful Vega wasn't here to see Sunny like this or he would'a irritated her. Then the two of them would'a started to conflict again. And I didn't want that.

"I'll see you in after-school," I told Sunny.

She smiled. Sunny seemed different.

After her and her sling had left, Joseph Marti and his girl Shonte ran through. But I had to break away from them to talk to my neighbor Steve Jenkins. He took one look at my face and asked if I'd been banging.

I shrugged.

He looked at me and sighed. I suddenly felt guilty, but didn't know why. The book he gave me at Christmas had really started all this. How Steve thought about me was important.

Steve had showed up with his girl too and was looking over my work very closely. He was quiet for a long while. "Lolly," he finally said. "This is amazing, Black man." His girl nodded.

"Thanks, man," I said. "There's a lot more to it, but I have to tear it down because they need the space. It was Mr. Ali's idea to put them on display out here today for the health cookout. Everything comes down tonight."

"That's messed up. So this is kind of a last hurrah," Steve said. I didn't know what that meant. "All of this is you, man?" he asked, nodding at the Legos.

"These two are all mine," I said, pointing. "The other two pieces were built by my friend Rose."

Steve raised his eyebrows. "Big-head Rose?"

I nodded.

Steve turned to his girl. "Rose is special-needs, his friend that helped build this," he told her. His girl's name was Rayshonne. She was nice. And nice-looking.

"It's lovely, Lolly," Rayshonne told me. "When Steve asked me to drop through, I wasn't expecting this. Dang, you got skills."

"This should be in a gallery," Steve said.

"Or online," Rayshonne added.

"Sharp idea, Candy Girl," he said to her. "Lolly, go stand next to Rayshonne near your masterpiece."

For the next twenty minutes, I posed with Rayshonne in front of our Lego bridge while Steve took pictures and videos. He videotaped me telling him what everything was about. It was like a real interview like you see on CNN, or something.

When I got to talking about Jermaine, I realized that I didn't feel as sad as I had been before. In a way, it was like this city was built for my brother.

Steve pulled me aside. "Your brother took that easy path," he said to me. "You're a hard worker. I see that. You don't wanna wind up like some of these *easy niggas*. You don't wanna do that again to your mother."

I started to say something, but didn't.

Steve told me to come to him, or anybody, if I had real problems. Before he left, he pointed at me and said, "Stay out of trouble."

· + + + ·

The best part of the day was showing my work to Daddy Rachpaul. He showed up alone. It was Saturday, so Daddy was on his way to a kids' party up in Riverdale. He came wearing most of his red-and-yellow Rocky the Clown makeup, saying he was in a rush.

I think he just liked wearing that makeup.

Again, Daddy analyzed the bruise on my face, first thing. He talked about enrolling me in a martial arts class. Or boxing.

Then he criticized Ma. "Sue-ellen made you soft. She still associate with that limp wrist Jonathan?"

"You know she do, Daddy," I said. "See what I made?" I pointed at my work.

I think he had expected something the size of when he had seen my castle on Late Christmas. These whole neighborhood sections were way bigger and more complex.

I'd grown.

His mouth dropped open. Just like how Vega's does when he's playing 'Ye.

"Wallace," Daddy said to me, "this is something fantastic, boy. The strength of artistry needed to construct all of this here. And the *vision...*" He scratched his chin. Flakes of red clown paint flicked the air. "Who would'a thought that all this could come from that itty-bitty tub of Legos we bought you years ago."

"It makes me happy," I said. "Makes me *me*."

At the end of the day, after everybody had left, Rose finally moped back.

I didn't ask where she had been or why she hadn't returned during the cookout. By now, I knew that she did stuff in her own way.

Crowds weren't really her thing, I figured.

While a few of the center staff and the DJ started to break down their equipment, Rose and me quietly went to work on our masterpieces. Without saying a word to one another, we started to deconstruct each of our city sections by chunks and bricks. Most of the pieces went back into the trash bags that Yvonne had delivered them in.

Rose and I both kept some.

It was my idea to give away most of the bricks to the

kids in St. Nick Houses. Mr. Ali said he would take care of delivering them. I mean, I couldn't keep them all, and it'd be better for all the kids at St. Nick to be able to use them and construct all kinds of junk with them.

Create their own worlds.

I had learned it was better to share your stuff. You get back more than you think you would. Mr. Ali had even said the center might sponsor a Harlem Lego champs Ten-Foot Tower Contest next year. And Rose and I could be the judges.

I liked his idea.

Back in the city room—or really the storage room now—we finished tearing down what was left of Rose's piece of Harlem and my alien world.

I was surprised by how fast it fell. The construction had taken so long. The destruction didn't last any time at all.

I guess it's quicker to tear down something than to build it up.

As I watched everything disappear, I felt both satisfied and gloomy. We had fixed so much pain into all of this. But we had learned a lot too.

And it had changed us.

Earlier that afternoon, when my father was checking out my masterpieces, I spoke something to him that I would'a never said before all this.

He knew about my phone getting ganked and offered to buy me a new one to replace it. He said to me, "Whatever you need, your pa, the foul-destroyer, is always here for you. Despite what your mother tell you."

I said to him, "I wish you'd been here when Jermaine needed you." Right away, I had felt bad saying it.

This seemed to make him deep-think, though.

Then he just said, "Do nah *buff* me, Wallace," meaning I shouldn't judge him. Daddy went on, "Do nah *buff* me. You can never surely know another man, son. Not truly. Your mum rejected me, tossed me outta yer lives. Blame her."

He took one last glimpse at my bridge and wiped the corners of his eyes. "This paint sticks darn near everywhere," he said, "buggin' me eyeballs."

Daddy hugged me swift.

"I'm late," he said, peeking at his watch.

He turned to leave, but I told him, "You didn't used to wear that face paint before you and Ma broke up. You never used to grin like I see you with your girlfriend. I don't think you were happy with Ma, Daddy. Maybe the two of you breaking up was better."

Daddy scratched his chin again. "*Maybe*, Wallace," he said, shaking his head. "I just wonder if your mum and me had stuck together, despite our problems, if things would'a gone better for Fox."

Fox was what my father used to call Jermaine because Jermaine had been so sly.

Daddy let out the biggest breath. "I'm late. I gotta *buss* it."

29

O n Monday I was walking home from after-school and passed by this car booming hip-hop near a building at St. Nick. I slowed down, but didn't stop, trying to pick out the kids crowded inside and outside the ride. There were lots of young dudes and pretty girls.

Frito and Chivonne were sitting in the backseat with the door open. Frito's cousins were leaning against the hood.

And sitting in the front passenger side was Vega.

Chillin'.

This pissed me off. So Vega didn't have time to come to my Lego show at the health fair, but had time to hang out chillin' with these folks?

He saw me looking at him and tried to get out of the car, but Frito pulled him back. Next thing, Frito was walking toward me on the sidewalk, looking around everywhere, pulling up his pants. For a second, I got a peek at the handle of a pistol, tucked into his waistband.

"Yo," he called to me. He pointed down the sidewalk. "Let's walk."

"A'ight," I said. I didn't feel like I had a choice.

Frito and me walked along the sidewalk for a minute, not saying nothing. He looked up at the trees. When we were far enough away from the car, he stopped and stared at me.

"I asked you to talk to Cas," he said.

"I hardly see him," I said. "Where he been? He missed the health show."

Frito rubbed the side of his face. "I heard. He been sick. He's okay now. Congratulations, man. Somebody sent me a link to your stuff."

"Thanks."

He nodded slowly. "Legos, huh?"

I glanced back to Vega, who was watching us. He looked nervous. Frito pulled me farther down the sidewalk.

"Vega didn't tell me he was sick," I said.

"He let Harper and Gully get at him. You know. In actuality, I am worried over my cousin, *manin*. *Both* of you, I'm worried over. This Harp and Gully thing—the East Side Squad." Frito shook his head.

"Why they want you to join they set so bad?"

Frito stopped walking. I stopped too. He pulled up his pants again and squinted.

"Well," Frito started. He stroked the couple of hairs on his chin and grinned. "Those boys, Loll, they want me to join in—because of how *nice* I am. But—*mi wanna do mi own ting!*" He laughed. "You got me, Trini?"

I grinned and laughed too. I didn't really get what he meant, but I didn't wanna make him mad. Frito was a good-looking dude with a smile that could make any girl do anything for him. But there was also something about that smile that made me nervous: it came and went too easy.

Frito leaned into my face. "I'm a shot caller, Trini. You would *want* to be down with *my* boys. You and my cousin. Think on it." He tapped the side of my head and turned me back around toward the car.

I told him I'd think on it. I didn't like looking over my shoulder every day.

"Think long," Frito said, "think wrong!"

I thought about Harp and Gully and how much I wanted to destroy them. They were forcing me into this choice. It was one I'd dodged and avoided for a long time.

But now . . .

"*¡Protección!*" Frito said, smiling one more time before we slapped hands.

"Damn, Lolly!" Daryl Reynolds shouted. "You got another hundred Likes on your page, man. You blowing up!"

I hated that I didn't have a phone of my own to see what he was talking about. I dropped my pencil and stopped studying about whole numbers to lean over the worktable.

I also hated that Vega wasn't here. It was the last day before spring break and he had been absent from school and after-school all week. Still missing in action.

I had even ran up to his apartment the day before, after seeing him hanging with Frito and his crew in front of St. Nick. I rang his doorbell but nobody answered. I wondered if Vega was in his room, playing quiet, when I rang, or even if he had come to the door and eyeballed me through the peephole.

Not saying nothing.

It felt weird.

The other day, walking back down the stairs to my place, I thought about how quiet and gone Vega had been. Me, at least I had all the excitement and stuff around my Legos. That had helped occupy my brain.

But what did Vega have? Besides thinking and thinking on how angry he was over what had happened?

Well, he *did* play 'Ye and got into his music.

But...

The screen on Daryl's phone now said I had over ten thousand followers. That was about ten thousand more than I had had before last weekend. I couldn't even believe it.

"Wait!" Quintesha yelled. She leaned over the table, twisting Daryl's phone so she could see. "Dang, Lolly! You a star!"

"'Tesha, sit back in your chair," Ms. Jenna said. She walked over to our table. "You kids cannot sit still."

"It's my Web page, Ms. Jen. I got over ten thousand followers. Just from last week."

Ms. Jen looked at me like I was silly. "Lolly, what are you talking about? Ten thousand followers? Why?"

"It's his Legos, Lady Bug," Daryl told her. "Everybody's liking 'em."

"Let me see that," Ms. Jen said. Daryl showed her. She raised her eyebrows and nodded. "Well, it's no surprise. We all loved Harmonee, Lolly. It was a wonderful thing. And that Maestro game? I'm not surprised to see how much everyone else loves it. You made something special."

"Then why'd you make him tear it down?" Quintesha asked with a scowl.

"That wasn't my call, 'Tesha," said Ms. Jen. "It wasn't up to me. But I'm glad to see it live on. Now, Daryl R., put that away. It's study time. And don't call me Lady Bug."

Daryl shoved his phone into his pocket. He whispered to me, after Ms. Jenna left, "You famous, Loll. *Too* cool, man."

I could barely consider it myself. I hadn't ever been recognized for nothing. And it *was* cool that if I did get famous for something, it would be for Harmonee.

· + + + ·

Lying on my back on my bed, I thumbed through some pages of *The Collected Works of Phillis Wheatley*. The poems hadn't been as boring as I thought they would, but today I was about to explode.

I was mad that Vega wasn't here for this. Him being how he had been lately was getting old. I hoped he wasn't hanging out with Frito too much. His cousin had a way of making bad situations worse.

I bounced up again from my bed.

I tossed the poetry book down and rushed to the other side of my room. I decided that the miniature turret that I had built in the city room and since moved up here to my bedroom was better off on a higher shelf.

Ma had said it was okay for me to leave some of my old city in my bedroom. Just as long as I didn't try to conquer the whole apartment like before.

I checked myself out in the mirror behind my door. I wished I didn't have such a high nose bridge. Or squinty eyes.

I read some more poems, but something on the ceiling caught my attention.

A water bug.

I hopped onto a chair and smashed the bug with my yellow flip-flop. I knew Ma wouldn't want them to videotape no bugs marching across our ceiling. I stood there, watching what was left of the bug as it twitched a bit, stuck to the bottom of the flip-flop.

Ma swung open my door. She stood there for a minute, smiling at me. She was as excited as I was. I flicked the dead bug into the wastebasket and fell back onto my bed.

"You tired, sugar?" she asked. "I know *I* am. Somebody better catch that rooster running around here. All that cock-a-doodle-dooin' at the crack'a dawn is messing with my rest."

Yesterday I saw a bunch of the building janitors chasing that scrawny red chicken around with nets. They couldn't catch it. That skinny little bird was a sprinter.

Our door buzzer rang. I sprang up. Ma held up her hand. "Sit. I'll get it."

She answered the door and it was the TV news crew right on time. A Spanish reporter from one of the local news shows wanted to interview me because of my Lego city and all of the attention it had got online.

When the cameraman was ready, I sat on my bed with lots of my Legos behind me, and me and the reporter, Connie, basically had a convo about what I had been doing.

Nervous, I rubbed the bruise above my eye. Ma had covered it in makeup. I stared down at my fingers that had just touched there; they were flaked with tan powder.

"So, Lolly, you have almost a quarter of a million followers online now," Connie the reporter announced.

"I'm more surprised than anybody," I answered.

"Why Legos, Lolly?" she asked.

I wanted to answer her, but I couldn't think of nothing.

My brain had froze. It felt like I had been sitting there for an hour, silent, before Ma spoke up.

"Say something, sugar!" Ma yelled. She was leaning in my door, behind the cameraman.

"Can you edit her part out?" I asked Connie, not wanting to look dumb on TV. I could hear Sunny and Vega dissing me already.

"Oh, *honey*," Connie said. "Don't you worry yourself. We will edit this to make you sound like the absolutely brilliant young man you are." She smiled. Her teeth were the *whitest*. "You're in good hands!"

"Why Legos?" I said to her. *"Um . . ."*

To be truthful, it had been a long time since I had really thought about why I loved building with Legos so much. Daddy had bought me my first Lego kit. A tub of regular-looking Legos.

Then when I was older, Jermaine had bought me an outer-space Lego kit for Christmas. A moon landing. I remember that Christmas because it was the first time my brother had used money that he had earned himself to buy us our Christmas gifts.

That was a big deal.

He had made that money from sweeping up the loose hair from that barbershop that used to be on St. Nicholas Av'. Years later, it was the shady dudes in that same gang that had recruited Jermaine to become a "street pharmacist."

He changed fast after that.

But that Christmas he had used his sweep-up money to buy us presents, and he was so proud. Daddy and Ma were too. Back then, we had all been expecting him to do excellent things later in his life.

That Christmas I think he had been feeling rotten about having told me to not hang around him no more. So he bought me a good present to make up for that.

Funny...

Last summer, before Jermaine got shot, he was lying on his bed over there. He was complaining about me having too many Legos all over our room. I listened to him, and then I asked him if he remembered buying me my first outer-space kit.

His face was blank. He couldn't remember.

I was shocked because, for me, it had been such a major deal. It stuck out in my memory; it was the reason I had got interested in telling space stories. But to him, he had forgotten it all.

That was how Prince Stellar, King Blaze, Queen Misteria, the Star Drivers and the Swarm and all of them had been born.

"Why Legos?" I repeated to Connie the reporter. She flashed me the whitest, teethiest smile. I took a deep breath and dove in.

30

Another nice day in April, and me and Rose were out. I tried to tell her about my TV interview yesterday, but she didn't act concerned. Some things she cared about—other stuff, not at all.

Today's trip was the middle of the week because we were on spring break. We'd been scouting for new buildings for me to sketch around the Meatpacking District downtown.

This part of town felt different, like we weren't in New York anymore. The streets under our feet were made of cool cobblestones. But on Washington Street we found a diamond.

For real.

Sitting on top of this normal brick building, there was the most amazing glass . . . thing. It was mostly made of windows, all jagged like the sections of a gigantic jewel, with what looked like steel beams holding it all together.

Somebody lived in that thing, I realized.

They had built themselves a crystal house on top of this ordinary building.

I was just about to take a picture of the diamond when I remembered that my phone had got stolen. And my tablet didn't take photos. It was lucky that Rose had her camera with her.

An old couple came out of a door on the building's street level. We asked them to snap a pic of us with the weird glass penthouse behind us. The old man was tall and bald and wearing a gray suit. His wife was real old too, but also pretty.

Her eyes were the biggest I'd ever seen and she had long brown hair. She pointed at my head and said, "I love your hat!"

I reached up to touch my African hat and straighten it. The tassels on top had started to frazzle.

"That's a nasty bruise," the old woman said, frowning at my forehead. "Do you like my tree house?" she asked us. She snapped our pic on the cobblestones. This lady had a funny accent, like she was from somewhere else.

"You live up there?" I asked.

"Live, work, love, make art," she said, and smiled. "It's my oasis. What do you think?"

"It's like a diamond," Rose blurted out, then gazed at the stone pavement. I was surprised she had spoke to a stranger.

The lady laughed. Her husband said to her, "You

certainly have enough of *those*." The woman looked at Rose like she was curious about her.

"You're interested in architecture, dear?" the wife asked.

Rose and I both nodded.

"Well, walk our High Line," the lady said, pointing behind us.

The husband then said to her, *"Diane?"*

She handed Rose back her camera and the couple were gone, hopping into a long black limousine.

The place where she had pointed was a city park hovering in the air. The High Line was not like any park I'd ever seen before.

The whole thing used to be an abandoned set of train tracks that ran through the Meatpacking District. The park was basically a straight line with a boardwalk and plants to make it pretty.

The coolest thing was that the whole park floated in the air!

Columns that reminded me of Lego blocks supported it. We had to climb up about two stories of steps to get to the High Line, but when we did, we had the most special view of the city all around us.

A high-class view.

And it was more peaceful up here than down on the

street. Suspended up two stories made all the city noise disappear. No motorcycles roaring or car horns. This could'a been somewhere in Harmonee, I thought.

It was the *best*.

I couldn't believe there wasn't a page on it in *A Pattern of Architecture*. I had started to wonder about how many other nice things we were missing that weren't in that book.

"We need more books," Rose said.

The two of us had sat down on one big wooden chair beside the boardwalk. I had bought each of us a bottle of water at a fancy food stand up here. I had wanted to buy some munchies at the stand, but all the food they sold was high.

I unpacked my sketchbook and looked around. There were lots of wild plants and interesting architecture here. It was like one big, long garden museum.

But I didn't think any of this had been built for me. I could imagine Diane and her rich husband strolling around up here, close to the clouds, but Rose and me were out of place.

"We do need more books for research," I said to Rose, after thinking on it for a while. "I want to make art. Like that woman Diane said. For the rest of my life. Until I'm old like her and still making art."

"That's good," Rose said, nodding. "I do too."

"Even if we don't know how to make it happen," I said.

She had spotted something. It was the head of a man

made out of metal. I had noticed a bunch of them scattered along the High Line. I guessed the metal heads were art, on display.

Yeah, they were definitely art, I decided.

This little redheaded girl was touching a metal head while her mother watched her. I wondered how different I would be if I'd grown up like that, surrounded by art all the time instead of Ma's Pez holders.

Were Pez holders art?

After that little girl had left, I touched the metal head too. It echoed when you knocked on it. I wondered how it was made, exactly.

Rose glugged the last of her water and asked, "You gonna make art out of Legos for the rest of your life?"

I paused, deep-thinking on this.

"I don't know," I said, moving my fingers over the metal.

Rose and me walked into my place after a long day stumbling around town. This was her first time over. It was weird having a girl in here.

I hoped Ma wasn't at home. Not because I wanted to try anything with Rose—she was just a friend—but I knew that if my mother saw that I brought a girl home, her and Yvonne would act all crazy.

"You want a fruit pop?" I asked Rose.

She shook her head. I could hear Michael Jackson singing "Got to Be There." It was coming from inside Ma's room.

"Well, let me show you my Lego shelves," I said to Rose. Rose started to follow me back to my room when I heard Ma yell out.

"Lolly!" Ma roared. "Sugar! I been waiting on you!"

Dressed in her pink fuzzy bathrobe, Ma came rushing out. She clenched one of her mystery novels under one arm. When Ma saw Rose standing in the hall, Ma stopped and clutched her bathrobe like she had just seen a mouse.

"Hello, Rose!" Ma said.

"Hello," Rose said. She smiled at the floor, looking embarrassed.

Ma looked at her strange, then snapped out of it. "I am so glad you are here, honey," she told Rose. "I got news for the both of you! You will *never* guess who called this afternoon!"

I stared at her, blank.

"Well, you ain't gonna guess?" she said.

"You just told me I could never guess who called," I said.

Rose giggled at this. My mother rolled her eyes.

"Stop being smart, funny boy!" Ma said. "Tuttle's! Tuttle's Toys!"

"Tuttle's?" I asked her. "The one at Rock Center where Yvonne works?"

"Mr. Tuttle!" Ma yelled. "The owner, Harold Tuttle

himself, called here today. He said he saw you and your Legos on the news last night."

"Oh yeah?"

"He was so impressed with what you and Rose built that he wants you two—*both* of you, Rose—to build him something for Easter, for the front window of his store! The big one down at Rockefeller Center!"

"Oh snap! We was just down there."

Ma went on, "And he's gonna pay you to do it! I bet Mohawk had something to do with this. That Yvonne probably got him to call you. Lolly! What do you think? You gonna do it? What you think?"

All I could do was smile. Rose was grinning at the floor. After a second, she covered her face with her hands.

"What *you* think, Ma!" I said.

Earlier today down at the High Line I had fantasized about living a life making art. And doing only that. But neither Rose or me knew how we could even start.

Now, without us even asking, somebody was gonna *pay* us to be real artists. It was just what we had wanted. Just what we had dreamed about.

I was sorry Vega wasn't here. I had asked him to come with us today, but he hardly ever came out of his apartment anymore.

But wait till I told him this!

I couldn't believe it.

31

I leaned back on Vega's bed and listened to him play his instrument. Closing my eyes, I pressed the ice-cold Snapple Apple bottle to the tiny bruise above my eye. I unscrewed the bottle's cap and swigged.

Out of all the sweet drinks that I liked, Snapple Apple was my all-time fave.

It tasted just like a real apple.

I sat my half-full bottle back down on Vega's nightstand. He was sitting on the edge of a chair, near his bedroom window, running the bow over his violin's strings. The book on violins that Steve had got him for Christmas was lying behind him on his windowsill.

It was good to be hanging out with him again.

Here it was, almost Easter, and so much had happened since Christmas.

I asked Vega if he would be spending summer down in DR—his favorite subject—and he didn't say nothing. Just shrugged and kept playing his violin.

This was something I had to get used to. Vega being quiet. Hardly saying nothing at all.

It was just freaky.

And very un-Vega.

He looked lonely and dejected.

I almost had to force my way in here today to see him. I should'a been more forceful about it sooner, but I guess I'd been so caught up in my own drama that it had been kind of hard.

Oh! I spoke to that dude Tuttle the other day. Me and Rose had called him back and talked with him. Well, I spoke to him, at least. Rose just sat next to me and listened, not saying nothing as usual.

Anyway, Tuttle went on and on about how much he loved seeing the videos and photos of our Legos and about how much talent Rose and me had.

I liked hearing that and liked talking with him. He seemed like a real chill dude and we spoke for a while.

I asked him if he knew Yvonne and he said yeah. He was surprised that I knew her.

And then, like Ma had said, he asked if me and Rose would like to come down to his store and build versions of our Lego cities for the front windows of Tuttle's Toy Emporium.

I swear my heart jumped.

Grinning like a little kid, I said yeah we would do it!

Though Rose still had to ask her grandmother. Tuttle said he wanted them built in time for Easter Sunday, and I told him that was plenty of time.

"We work fast, Mr. Tuttle!" I said. "Especially Rose. We're professional."

"I just bet you are, Lolly," he answered back over the phone. "You two young people have crafted beautiful thinga-majigs. Just lovely things. We'll work out the payment details when I see you."

"That's no big deal, Mr. Tuttle. Rose and I'd do it for free! . . . *Ow!*"

Ma had poked me in my side after hearing me say that. Tuttle just giggled. We agreed that we'd come down next Saturday to get started, once Rose had talked to her gran.

The first thing I did today when I saw Vega was tell him all about it. He listened about Tuttle's Toys and Rock Center and new Lego cities and becoming real artists, and then he gave me a weak smile and said, "That's smooth, *manin.*"

And then he had started playing his violin. He had been playing up until now, when he had finally finished his song.

I clapped loud, thinking about what kind of city we would build at Tuttle's.

Maybe Harmonee?

Or something new?

Maybe we could build something together again. . . .

After I had finished clapping, it was quiet in his bed-room for a minute. I watched him stare at 'Ye. He seemed to see something stuck to the back of it and picked at the spot until it rubbed off.

"Casimiro Vega!" I shouted. I felt myself trying to give him some energy, a good mood. Just like he does for me whenever I feel down about Jermaine.

He continued to weak-smile me. I sat up.

"You can keep a secret?" Vega asked.

"What's up?" I asked.

He carefully leaned his violin against the wall and stood. 'Ye slid to the side and plopped to the floor.

"¡Coño!" Vega shouted. He grabbed his instrument and lightly placed it beside me and knelt down on his rug to pull a shoebox out from under the bed.

Inside that box was a black Glock. At first, I thought it was a toy gun, but I could tell by the way he handled it that it was real. Without saying nothing, he passed it to me, handle first.

In my palms, it weighed heavy. And it was real cold.

I didn't know what Vega wanted me to do with this gun. I was wondering what *he* had planned to do with it when the idea suddenly popped into my head.

He had been acting funny ever since Harp and Gully had jumped us at Manny's bodega. Plus they had already ganked Vega's new coat that he had loved so much.

"They need to feel this," Vega said toward the gun in my hands. He looked at me. "They need to be scared."

I quickly handed the heaviness back to him. I had suddenly felt like that Glock had infected me with something.

Or maybe it had been Vega?

Before I had come up here to visit him, I had felt better. Hoping for a life maybe making art.

Now, watching him stare at that gun . . . Something had tickled at the center of my chest again. It was still tiny, the size of a speck of sand, but I knew it could grow as heavy and as mean and as cold as that gun.

We both sat there, hypnotized.

"I got it from Frito," Vega said, whispering. "For Harp, Gully."

I massaged the bruise above my eye. It had almost disappeared, but had started to throb again. Or maybe I had just started to concentrate on it.

"You crazy," I said. I shook my head. "You really think we could do that? We ain't Frito."

"I could," Vega said. "I guess."

"Hit Harp and Gully?" I shook my head, not because we couldn't do it, but I had trouble actually picturing us doing it. But Jermaine had told me once that anybody could do anything, if they had a weapon and a reason to use it.

"*Mira*," Vega said. "I been thinking all over this. Plus Frito told me if I get Harp and Gully, we won't have to worry then. His crew will protect us, *manin*. And Frito takes over *their* crew. Because Harp and Gully wouldn't . . . well, you know . . . well, that's what Frito told me."

I watched Vega kneel there on the floor beside his bed, staring at his Glock. His face had got limp now all of a sudden. Like he felt hazy, lost in a dream.

Vega said, "We'd just have to let them find us again. Like they do. It'd be easy. That's what Frito said."

It'd be easy.

That's what Jermaine had said too.

Rockit thought he knew what Jermaine had wanted for me. A better life.

What did stupid Rockit know anyway?

Him saying Jermaine wanted me to study and go to college . . . Rockit didn't know. Nobody knew nothing.

"I think it was my fault, Vega," I mumbled.

"No!" Vega yelled. "Harp and Gully mess with everybody. They don't care—"

"No, man. I'm talking about Jermaine."

Vega's eyes grew wide. I slid from his bed down to the carpet.

"Just before Jermaine got shot up," I started, "me and him hadn't been speaking at all—at least, not for that whole week before he died. We had had a argument. A big one that had got him real upset with me. I had wanted to talk to Jermaine after that, but he hadn't really wanted to associate with me."

"Why was you two beefin'?" Vega asked.

I remembered back to just before Halloween. The same argument that Mr. Ali had been trying to get me to speak about during our talks. I had never told it to anybody.

Not even my best friend.

"Vega, for days Jermaine had been trying to convince me to join his crew. The stuff they used to do down at the barbershop?"

Vega nodded.

I went on. "Jermaine said he could get me on there, so I could have some money in my pocket and him and me could work together. He said it'd be *easy*, what they would have me doing—just little stuff like running packages from one spot to another, dropping off money from one place to another. Easy stuff. But I didn't wanna do it. Because of what Ma would say and how she might think of me."

My eyes were getting wet. I stared Vega in his eyes now.

"Years ago, when I was little," I said, "he had made me promise that I would never do it. That I'd stay away from his barbershop. And not let *nobody* talk me into doing any of that. . . . But before he died, Jermaine had stopped talking to me because he said he had gone out of his way to try to bring me on there and me refusing was making him look weak. Foolish."

"Lolly," Vega said. *"Man . . ."*

I shook my head. "I let Jermaine down. I let him down,

Vega." I leaned forward onto my knees. "I should'a been there."

"Maybe he was right, Loll," I heard Vega whisper. He ran his hand over the gun's barrel. "Things were different when we was little. Nobody'd mess with us. We ain't little no more. It ain't safe."

We sat quiet for a minute.

"You really think we should do that?" I asked.

"We need to man up, Loll."

We both stared at the gun, lost in it. Lips moving, Vega seemed to be reading something written on it: words that weren't there, but he could see them just as plain.

I knew whose names he saw there.

I could almost read them too.

32

"**L**olly!"

"What!"

"Get out here!" Ma called. "You got company!"

Company?

I sat up on my bed. It couldn't be Vega; he wouldn't leave his bedroom and his Glock—his new best friend.

Ever since yesterday, when Vega had showed me the gun that Frito had got for him, I had noticed that everything was pissing me off. All of a sudden it seemed like everybody and their cousin had started to irritate me.

I wasn't feeling right.

In the past day, I didn't know how many times I had planned out what was going to happen to Harp and Gully. Just thinking about this made me different, feel how I *used* to feel.

I shuffled through the living room and heard voices in the kitchen. One was my mother's voice. The other one was a girl's voice. Not Rose's, but . . .

I turned the corner into the kitchen and saw Ma and Sunnshyne Dixon-Knight sitting there at the small table. I gulped and folded my arms over my chest. Though I was wearing a superhero T-shirt and pajama bottoms, I suddenly felt like I was undressed.

Sunny looked at me and smiled. She was still wearing her arm in her sling.

"Hey, Lolly!" she said.

Ma stood up and gave me a strange look. The same kind of look she had gave me when she first met Rose in our apartment.

"Little Sunnshyne brought you something," Ma said, walking out the kitchen. Before Ma left, she stopped and told me, "You two stay out here, you hear me?" She gave me that look again, then turned back toward Sunny. "Baby, I don't want you back in his bedroom. It's so filthy in there, you might catch something."

Ma laughed at this in one big chirp and left us alone. I stayed there in the doorway, pinching the side of my neck.

"They still ain't caught Harper and Marq Gully," Sunny said. She shook her head and played with the foil covering an aluminum baking pan. "Thugs."

"What's that?" I asked her about the pan.

Sunny had brought it over filled with these pastelles she had made. She told me she had baked them for me during this week off from school. With Butteray Jones's help.

Her cooking coach, I guess.

I nibbled one of her pastelles. It wasn't very good. In fact, it was nasty, but I didn't say nothing. I just swallowed and fought back regurgitating.

Sunny looked at me, all anxious. I smiled at her and grabbed a can of seltzer water from the refrigerator.

It was weird eating pastelles in April. We only ever had them around Christmas. But Sunny wouldn't know that. Her family wasn't from the Caribbean. They weren't *coconuts* like me and Ma.

"You like it?" Sunny asked.

I nodded, glugging down water. "Butteray taught you how to make 'em, huh?"

She nodded and smiled at the floor. "He's not my boyfriend, you know. He likes dudes."

"I figured," I said, swallowing more seltzer, trying to get that taste out of my mouth.

"Oh, he's cool. I like him. Mama works at Aunt Cushie's. Ray learned to cook real good from his parents. They're both chefs."

I swallowed the last of my water.

Sunny went on, "At first, I didn't like him—Butteray. We fought a lot, like you and me used to. But now Ray and I are friends. Just like me and you. I gotta go." She stood up fast.

"I told Mama I'd drop these off and come right back home."
Sunny started to leave.

"How'd you hurt your arm?" I asked her at our front
door. "Butteray?"

"Oh no! Ray'd never do that! He's nice."

"You sure? He acts weird. . . ."

She looked embarrassed and opened the door. "I think,
for some reason, Ray was scared that I *liked* him. You know.
Ain't that dumb? Why would I like a boy who likes boys? I
don't know how he got that dumb idea."

Sunny was lying, I could tell. She *had* liked Butteray.
I bet she didn't know about him and now she felt stupid
about it.

I could'a told her he was *one of the children*. That was
Ma's slang for gay people. Growing up around them, I could
sometimes spook who was who. By "spook," I mean *recognize*.

"Stupid April E. did this to my elbow," Sunny said. "Well,
not on purpose. We were trying to rescue a coyote—"

"That one in St. Nicholas Park?"

"Yeah! You saw him too? His name is Nicky. April and I
spotted him in the park one day and we had been trying to
catch him before the police did. We were afraid they'd shoot
him, or something."

"Me too!" This girl was something else, I thought.

Sunny checked her phone for the time, walked across

the hall and pressed the elevator down button. She walked back over to me, standing in my doorway.

"I think he's still out there," Sunny whispered. "In the park. I haven't seen him in a while, but I know they didn't catch him. It'd be on the news if they had. April and I had been trying to tempt Nicky out with chicken runts. April's cousin at Eastside Poultry gave them to us."

"That's where you two were coming from the night we got jumped?"

"Yeah. But way after that we were chasing down one of those dumb birds and I fell backward on my butt and my arm got twisted between April's big fat thighs."

"Ouch," I said.

"Yeah," she said. "Dislocated elbow. Not that serious. She needs to lose weight."

"What were you gonna do with the coyote—Nicky?" I asked. "If you caught him."

She shrugged. Her black braids swung up into the air with her shoulders. I heard the elevator ding behind her.

I asked her again, "But didn't you guys think about what might happen?"

"Sometimes, Wallace," she started, "you just do what you know is right, even if it seems dumb at the time."

Sunny pecked me quick on the knot above my eye and disappeared into the elevator.

Ding!

I watched her smile vanish between the closing doors. Where her lips had touched me felt hot.

· ✦ ✦ ·

Spring break was almost over.

I wasn't looking forward to going back to school and after-school. I just didn't feel like it. And I knew Ali would be bothering me again about us talking.

I was done talking with him.

Stepping off my bike, I peered into St. Nicholas Park for any signs, but didn't see none. I stood there at the edge for a minute, looking into all the green there.

Was Nicky the coyote really still here?

Sunny sure thought so.

I thought about its glowing eyes and shivered and remembered how scared the coyote had made us that night.

I reached into my backpack. Sunny's pastelles were there, wrapped in aluminum foil. I placed them on a nearby wooden park bench, painted green and flaking.

I backed away and hopped back onto my bike. I wondered if coyotes with glowing yellow eyes liked pastelles as much as they liked French fries. Before I left, I took another peek through the trees and into the park.

Our coyote was nowhere.

Disappeared.

Like everything else does sooner or later. Nicky was gone. Like Harmonee. Like Jermaine.

I was getting angry again and couldn't help it.

Vega and his gun had really infected me.

My chest had gotten heavier.

Just like before.

33

Ma had fried chicken for our dinner. With that, we also had some carrots and peas, which I usually liked a lot. I sipped from another bottle of Snapple Apple, but wasn't eating nothing.

I didn't feel like it.

All I could think about was Jermaine and about Vega's gun and what we were gonna do with it. I still felt guilty about saying no to what my brother had asked.

I knew I had let him down. Vega was right. We weren't safe. Any time we could go out just like my brother.

"Funny boy, you gonna eat that food," Ma said to me. She took a bite of a drumstick and then used a paper towel to squash a roach that had crawled out hoping to get at some of her dinner.

They got strong noses, roaches, I heard.

"Food is hard enough to come by, without you wasting what I cook," she said. "If I brought Moses in here from off the street, I bet he'd love this chicken."

What did that old bum Moses have to do with anything?

I scooped some peas and carrots into my mouth to shut her up.

"I wonder where's Yvonne?" Ma asked nobody, really.

We had waited a whole hour for Yvonne to drop by after work like she usually did on Tuesdays. But even after that, she still hadn't showed, so Ma decided for us to go on and eat without her. Yvonne wasn't answering her phone either.

"Not like Yvonne to miss my chicken," Ma told her plate. "She loves my chicken."

"Yeah," I said with a sigh. It *was* strange, though.

"Peculiar," Ma said.

In my mind I was running over and over again the scene of me and Vega walking down 125th Street. In my dream it was late at night. On a Friday. It was just me and Vega walking all slow and then Harp and Gully jump out from behind the statue of Adam Clayton Powell.

You know, the statue with his coat fluttering behind him like a cape?

Yeah, so in my mind, Harp and Gully jump out at us. But this agitates neither me or Vega. We *hard.*

"You two little punks better be *skeered*," one of them goes. Probably Harp.

Then Vega yanks out his violin. But his violin is made all out of Legos.

Harp and Gully laugh, teasing about how weak Vega is

for playing a Lego violin. And they just stand there laughing while Vega plays this real beautiful, sad song on Lego 'Ye. Just like the song he was playing the other day in his bedroom.

This song is so beautiful that it makes Harp and Gully weep over how beautiful it is. They straight-up start to sob.

And then, just when Vega is playing the most beautiful part of his song, he points 'Ye at both of them and plucks one last note.

Bang!

His violin shoots out a black bullet straight into Harp's forehead and the bullet keeps flying straight into Gully's forehead, right behind Harp!

They both drop to the pavement dead. And their bodies break all apart into little blocks.

They were made of Legos!

Me and Vega keep on down 125th. He starts playing a new song. Both of us is, like, *"What!"*

I chuckled, sitting at the kitchen table.

"What's amusing?" Ma asked.

Her phone, sitting beside her on the table, started to buzz. From where I sat, I could see Yvonne's upside-down selfie grinning on the front of the phone. She was finally calling to say why she was so late. This ought to be entertaining.

"Where you at, Mohawk?" Ma said, answering her phone. I could tell she was about to get into Yvonne.

"Mmm-hmm," Ma said into the phone. She sucked her teeth, shaking her head. "Well, don't bother coming over here tonight. Lolly and me ate up all the supper. We finally caught that ghetto chicken that's been running around here." She winked at me and smiled. "Of *course* I'm joking, girl," Ma said into her phone.

My mind floated loose.

The only thing that I could concentrate on now was getting Harp and Gully. I had just started to daydream again about another scene with me and Vega going after them when Ma shouted out so loud it made me jump.

"What!" she yelled into her phone. "Arrested?" Ma went on. Now I was paying attention. "Yvonne," she said, "what did you do?"

Ma listened to her for a minute.

Then she frowned.

And frowned some more.

"Lolly?" she said into her phone.

Ma's eyes met mine and I suddenly felt guilty though I didn't even know why. I suddenly felt like she knew exactly what I'd been daydreaming about just then.

Revenge.

Sitting across from her at the table, I wondered if she knew what Vega and me had been considering to do with our gun. Like maybe they had even found it in his shoebox upstairs.

I knew that was crazy, but by the way my mother stared at me with her mouth hanging open, I could tell whatever this news was, it was gonna be *hostile*.

· + + + ·

It *was* bad.

Really bad.

And the evilest part was, I was sure the police would come to arrest me next. And they would arrest Ma too. Like we was all in it together. I figured we were all at risk of getting locked up.

We were already at the police station. The one down at 123rd and St. Nick Av'. Ma and me had been sitting in the waiting room at the Twenty-Eighth Precinct cop station in Harlem.

This was where they had taken Yvonne.

The cops had her back there in lockup right now with me and Ma waiting in this room out front. Right when you entered the station, there was this room with a desk where a cop sat behind. There were all these hard-as-hell chairs for the public to sit.

And wait.

Every now and then cops came in and out. Nobody ever looked at me and Ma sitting here. Like they didn't see us.

I had never been in here before. But when I was little,

me and my friends used to think this police station looked like a moon base. As little kids we used to pretend that.

From the outside it was shaped funny, like something that should'a been on another planet.

When I got older, I grew to know what it really was.

Me and Ma had been waiting the longest time—it was after midnight now—watching the police start to haul in all these other types they had busted.

I was hoping those two cops that gave me and Vega a ride home wouldn't show their faces.

Ma was wrecked.

The most messed-up thing she told me was that she remembered coming to this same police station to pick up Jermaine after he had got arrested years ago. She said she had felt like she'd failed him.

"Like I wasn't a good mother," she told me. Ma scrunched her face and sat up straight in her chair. These seats were cramped. "That night I picked your brother up from here, he said for me not to worry about him."

"Did you believe him?"

She sighed. "I told him then that I never wanted to be back at this place again. And that I was trusting in him. What I was also thinking, and hoping too, was that I never wanted to be in here with you, Lolly." She shook her head. "*Never.* Not sitting in here."

"At no time will you bail me out, Ma. I promise."

She gazed at me, heartbroken. But it wasn't just sad. I could tell in her face that she was also kinda deciding if she would believe me.

Ma's face.

Waiting on Yvonne at this cop shop. Her afraid this would be me one day. That really did it.

I could feel it.

Later that night, closer to one in the morning, I had fell asleep, leaning my head on Ma's big shoulder. We both were still sitting in those hard plastic chairs when there was a big crash. I shook awake and Ma jumped to her feet.

The cops had been lifting some young dude through the front doors and he had fell, I guess. Making a big racket.

Handcuffed and Black, he landed on the floor, right in front of us. Kinda heavyset. I couldn't see his face, but something about him was familiar.

He was breathing heavy, on his knees.

"Get up!" one of the cops yelled at him.

He stayed kneeling on the floor, face pointed at the tiles. He was heaving now. Like he was about to throw up.

Dude stared up at us. Ma and me just looked at him. He was, like, twenty-something. Face miserable. He stared at us like he needed help.

"Man, will you get up!" the cop shouted.

"Push me again and see what happens," the dude in handcuffs said. His voice was cracked.

"You need to watch where you step," the cop answered. "Up, up, up!"

The man shut his eyes and spat on the station floor.

Both police looked fed up. One pulled his nightstick out and twirled it. It was a long shiny rod.

Scowling, Ma raised her hand and shouted at the cop. "Why you wanna hit him?" That cop's stick stopped in the air, and him and his partner glanced at me and Ma and the cop behind the desk, who looked like this was just any other night.

It was like they was seeing us for the first time.

"I am an officer of the court," Ma said, exaggerating. "You only carry nightsticks when you wanna use 'em. I know that!"

She was right. I hardly ever saw the police carry those long sticks around anymore. Most of them used the expandable ones.

The two officers exchanged looks. The one clipped his baton back into his belt.

"Mind your business," he told Ma.

She sucked her teeth.

Loud.

Then they stepped to either side of the dude on the floor,

yanked him to his feet and dragged him into the back, where all the other people who got busted were laid up.

Before they disappeared, one of the police said, "He's been mixing it up all night."

I didn't know if he had meant that for us or the cop behind the desk. I didn't have much time to wonder on this, because right then the desk cop spoke up. "You two can go home. It says here Yvonne Grayson was sent down to Central Booking to see a judge."

"Central Booking?" Ma said. "When was this? We been here since—"

"Go home, lady," the cop said. "You won't see her tonight. They'll let her go late tomorrow." His phone rang. "If you're lucky."

34

The news really was hostile. It wasn't just my imagination.

My mother had her friend Mr. Jonathan—who worked at Legal Aid down at the courthouse—get us a lawyer to give us some advice.

This morning we had got up early, dressed up nice and took the subway down to Midtown, 47th Street. Thanks to Ma, we rose up out the subway on the wrong side of the street. I had tried to tell her she had picked the wrong exit, but she wouldn't listen. I had learned my way around because of my trips with Rose.

Today Ma was as nervous as I was. Probably even more.

Ma and me crossed over Sixth Av.' Rose and me had just been over here a few weeks ago when we had come to visit Yvonne at her job.

That day was fun. This day was evil.

My book bag's straps had started to slide down off my

shoulders. I hiked it back up, remembering what I'd brought inside it.

I gazed up at the tall buildings of Rockefeller Center. They calmed me some.

Ma and I marched to 50th and Sixth Avenue, where we had arranged to meet the Legal Aid lawyer. His name was Aston Stewart. Ma said that Aston sounded like a girl with a deep voice when she had spoke to him over the phone, but he was truly a dude.

"Probably *one of the children*," Ma had said.

As we approached Radio City Music Hall, where Aston was supposed to be, I spooked him out before he had even noticed us. Sure enough, even from half a block away, I could see plain as day that Aston was one of the children.

"I think that's him, Ma," I said, and pointed.

He saw me and smiled with a wave. He was waiting beneath that big Art Deco overhang at Radio City. This place for concerts was also part of Rock Center. When we stepped under that overhang, it blocked out the sun.

Aston was a tall, thin Black dude with a shaved baldy. He looked about Jermaine's or Steve's age but must'a been older. He was wearing these big black thick-rimmed glasses like that movie dude Spike Lee and was dressed all in black.

Except that what he was wearing was kind of in between what you would expect a man to wear and what you might expect a woman to wear. He wasn't wearing no dress or nothing like that, but he had on some skin-tight black leggings and a black kind-of poncho. His shoes were black too, with these jumbo silver buckles.

Ma's eyes bugged when she met him. Then she caught herself and shook his hand.

"Sue-ellen," Aston said. "Thanks for being on time!"

He was lively. And he had a nice smile. A smile that had put me at ease, as nervous as I had been. I liked what he was wearing, though I would never wear it myself. It made him stand out.

Unique.

"Mr. Stewart, thank you for coming with us and setting up this meeting," Ma said. "With everything that's happened, well..."

"Yes, yes, I know, *hon*," Aston said. His voice was deep for somebody dressed like he was. "Anything for a friend of Jonathan's. I just hope this Tuttle character doesn't *try* it."

By "try it," Aston meant: try to take advantage of us. Years of listening to how gay people talk had taught me a few things.

"You must be little Lolly," he said, turning to me.

"Hi," I said.

"Hello!"

"And it's just Lolly. Not little Lolly."

"Super! Well, I am so sorry this happened to you, Lolly.

But keep your head up." He glanced at his watch. "Let's go. I hate being tardy."

A woman met the three of us at the front door of Tuttle's Toy Emporium. She led us to an elevator in the back of the store behind the giant Lego dragon. We waited for the elevator. None of us said anything.

On either side of us were all these girl dolls, smiling, dressed in pink-and-white gowns. I felt like they were grinning at me. Teasing me. Aston scowled at them.

The inside of the toy store seemed louder and brighter than before. So that it kind of hurt my eyes and ears being here. Everything was more real this time.

Mr. Tuttle's office was empty.

It wasn't a really big office like I had thought it would be. It was kind of dark and coldish and it felt like we were in somebody's attic.

While me, Ma and Aston waited in three green-velvet chairs, Aston peeked at his watch. He mentioned again how much he hated people being late.

Ma just grunted.

She was comical sitting there in one of the two dresses she owned. She didn't like wearing dresses at all. Said they made her feel naked and vulnerable. I thought that I finally understood what she had meant.

Aston got up and poured himself a glass of ice water from a pitcher. The lady who had showed us into Tuttle's office had said to help ourself, but Ma and me didn't want none.

Our lawyer sipped his water and crunched an ice cube between his teeth. With his hand on his chin, Aston squinted, scanning Tuttle's office, taking in everything like he was studying a textbook.

"I wonder what compels a fully grown man to surround himself with playthings," he said.

Ma flared her nostrils at me, like I should know the answer. It seemed like Aston liked hearing himself talk even if nobody else was really listening.

"Maybe," I started, "maybe he likes to collect toys." Aston raised an eyebrow at me. I said, "If you're grown and own a toy store, that gives you an excuse to have a bunch of toys around you. Without people criticizing you."

"You think he plays with those frilly dolls downstairs?" Aston asked.

I shrugged. "You know how little kids get when you take their toys from them. . . ."

He grinned and crunched another chunk of ice between his teeth, then glanced at the door to the room. There were voices outside, coming nearer.

"*Showtime,*" Aston said. He sat the glass of water on a table and folded his hands behind his back. I glanced at my book bag between my legs on the floor.

Into the room walked two men. One old and the other one older. The older one said to the old one, "Well, we'll just have to wait and see, won't we?"

I recognized Harold Tuttle's voice right away. They paused at the door to eyeball Aston, Ma and me. Ma stood up. So did I.

Both men stared at Aston like they were analyzing somebody on the east side of 125th Street, trying to decide whose gang he belonged to.

Aston paced the small attic office. His black poncho-thing drifted behind him like a shawl.

"Mr. Tuttle," Aston went on. "All of us in this room know that Yvonne Grayson stole your toys—your Legos—from you. You must have felt troubled, betrayed, by this. But you've seen all of the good that came from Grayson's admittedly unjustifiable act."

After having gone back and forth with Aston for fifteen minutes, Tuttle finally waved his wrinkled hand at him like he was trying to shoo away a fly.

The other man, who had introduced himself as Rich Fowler, the vice president and legal counsel, but who Tuttle had introduced as his assistant, had been mostly quiet, leaning against the window behind his boss.

Tuttle's frosty office had got hot.

Aston continued, "Little Lolly's Lego cities were on the news. All over the Web. People across the planet have enjoyed the magic this impoverished child of Harlem created. Magic that originated from here—from *your* Legos, Mr. Tuttle."

Mr. Fowler rolled his eyes.

"Mr. Tuttle, what I'm saying is this: Sure, Yvonne Grayson stole from you. It's not too late for my clients to return to you all that was taken. But instead of prosecuting the Rachpauls, couldn't you regard this small incident as not one of thievery, but of *sharing*? Sharing your wonderful toys with this young boy who has so little and with the children of St. Nicholas Houses."

"My foot!" Tuttle blurted.

"I watched the Lego videos he shot in Harlem," Fowler added. "In one of them he mentions getting a new game console for Christmas."

"I did not buy that set for him!" Ma said. "It was that hoodlum Rockit." Aston shot her a look.

"Doesn't sound impoverished to me," Fowler said. "Or innocent, actually."

I grabbed my book bag off the floor. Fowler glanced at me.

"Mr. Stewart," Fowler said to Aston. "It is *mister*, isn't it?"

Aston narrowed his eyes.

Fowler continued, "You know that we have a signed confession from our *former* employee Yvonne Grayson. Yvonne admits stealing Legos from our store—God only knows how many—to give to her friend's son here." He nodded toward me. "They were all in on it."

"That ain't true!" Ma yelled. "She told me they were rubbish."

"And you *truly* feel that Ms. Rachpaul and her young *child* were complicit?" Aston asked him.

I felt small.

"Coercing Ms. Grayson in some way?" Aston went on.

"Why not?" Fowler asked.

Tuttle shook his head, then spoke in his quiet voice. "That woman has worked here for five years. She *had* worked here, I mean. I treated Yvonne the same as my, my grandniece Evelyn, or Richie here. Like *family*. Stealing from me!" he mumbled, almost trembling.

"Ms. Grayson's apologized and agreed to pay restitution, Mr. Tuttle," Aston said. "I don't exactly understand why we're here today."

"Wait a minute. This get-together was your idea, not ours," Fowler said.

"Yes," Aston answered. "Because you were threatening charges against my clients here. Charges that are groundless."

Tuttle straightened up in his chair and glared at me and

my mother. "Did you two ask Ms. Grayson to steal my merchandise for those Internet videos?"

I felt mad all of a sudden. "You mean, are we *crooks*?" I asked, kind of loud.

All heads turned toward me.

I took a deep breath and clutched my bag tighter. I tried to settle down. "My mother and I might not have much, but we don't need to steal."

I could feel myself getting angrier.

Tuttle started to speak, but I broke in, more quiet: "There's lots of stuff I want, Mr. Tuttle, but you won't see me being a hoodlum for any of that. Actually... seeing all the badness Yvonne caused taught me something extra— not how to do anything crooked, but just the opposite. I like using my head, building."

Tuttle didn't say nothing. I tried to recall how those lines went.

Then I remembered: "'Imagination, who can sing your force? Who can describe the swiftness of your course?'" I thought I had said that right. I rubbed my head. "That's Phillis Wheatley. I read that."

"I know Wheatley," Tuttle mumbled.

"*Well*," I said, feeling cooler, "it's about using your head, getting a spark from being creative, I think. All I'm trying to say is I'm *real* lucky that Yvonne helped me the way she did."

I had got too emotional.

"It saved me," I said.

I reached deep into my book bag. I felt around inside. I yanked out what I was looking for, clutching it in my hand.

Aston stood up straight, squinting at me.

I handed Tuttle the envelope I held. He read my message inside. In the letter, I had promised to work for him after school at Tuttle's Toys as a janitor, or whatever, until the money for the stolen Legos had been paid.

Tuttle was stupefied.

You don't really know anybody, or what they're capable of.

Aston almost spoke, but snapped shut. He folded his hands behind his back and waited. Tuttle was blinking at my letter in his hands. Fowler's eyes had wandered out the window.

Ma touched my hand with a pressed smile.

"One man's trash is another man's treasure," Tuttle finally mumbled in his weak voice. Fowler asked him what he had said. "Never mind, Richard," Tuttle told him. Then, to me, "I believe you, Lolly, that you had nothing to do with our pilfered Legos."

Ma let out a big sigh. Aston smiled and gave me a thumbs-up.

Tuttle announced, "I've decided, just now, to drop this matter and *not* press charges against Ms. Grayson." Behind him, Fowler groaned. "Richard, you will sweep this whole *thingamajig* under the rug for me. I am sapped."

"Yes, sir."

"Thank you, Mr. Tuttle!" Ma said, looking released. "We will return to you all of those Legos that are left. Some of them have been given away already."

Tuttle waved his hand at her. "Unnecessary, Mrs. Rachpaul," he said.

"The cost of sterilizing them would be prohibitive," Fowler added.

Mr. Jonathan would'a called him saying that "shady." Aston rolled his brown eyes at Fowler.

"And, Lolly," Tuttle said, "though we appreciate your offer to work off the cost of the Legos, that won't be necessary either. Focus on your schoolwork instead." He turned toward Ma. "Your son's an unconventional sort of young man, Mrs. Rachpaul."

"He's a little different," Ma said. "Like his mother."

"I see why Yvonne wanted to help him," Tuttle admitted. "However, her actions were *wrong*. We will not rehire her."

"Oh, we understand that," Ma said to Tuttle.

"And of course, I'll have to cancel my offer for the children to construct a decoration for our store," Tuttle said. "But I hope they keep on building."

Somebody knocked on his door. "Yes!" Tuttle shouted. "What is it, Ev?"

The young lady who had met us downstairs earlier cracked the door. Tuttle's next appointment, a toy exporter from China, was waiting on him outside his office.

"Thank you, Ev," Tuttle told the lady, then said to me, "I am fond of the old poems." He paused and told Ev, "Will you show the Rachpauls out? We're done."

35

I t was late at nighttime and me and Vega were roaming the streets of Harlem. Not many others were hanging out on the blocks. My eyes kept darting around in the darkness. I was waiting for Harp and Gully or some cops to pop up any second.

Seeing some movement up ahead, I motioned for Vega to pick up his step. I could just see two people up ahead on the street, but couldn't tell if it was the two older boys or not. Two shadows moved toward us.

Vega started faster toward them. I could tell that his hand was tightening around the gun in the pocket of his dark-blue hoodie.

My heart was booming like a woofer.

When we got to the end of the block, Vega and me could see their faces. It wasn't Harp and Gully. It was a young couple, a girl and a boy, walking real slow on their way somewhere.

Vega and me turned onto Macombs Place and walked across a long footbridge. We crept beside Rucker Park down below and stopped on a dark overlook, just across the river from the Bronx.

We had been leaning there against the wall for over twenty minutes. Our backs were to the Harlem River. Glancing over my shoulder, I could see the lights of Yankee Stadium across the water and Harlem River Drive beside us, traffic humming like bumblebees.

"You finally ready to do this?" I asked Vega.

He nodded. I stuck out my hand and he lightly placed the gun into it. I felt it in the darkness.

Heavy, cold and mean. That Glock felt like the end.

I leaned there against that wall, deep-thinking about Harp and Gully's faces and what they would'a done if they had been here right now.

What *we* would'a done.

I handed the pistol back to Vega.

He waited a second, then swung around and hurled that gun out into the night air, screaming. He had pitched it like he was throwing all of his fear and anger along with it. It flew about ten yards and disappeared into the Harlem River. I heard a *plunk* as it broke the water's surface.

He stood there a minute, watching the river rush by. I hoped that whatever rock Vega had been carrying in him had just sunk to the bottom of the river along with his gun.

The thing that really scared me and had brought me around was the night Yvonne got arrested. After she had called Ma on the phone, and we had walked over to the police station where they had her.

Ma's face had made something true for me. From that whole Yvonne experience and looking back at Jermaine too, my rock was gone.

I wouldn't *let* it grow back.

I think I was able to help Vega when I told him he had a choice to make too: Frito and the gun, or me and his violin.

I reminded him about Steve and Jermaine, growing up together, but parting ways. If he chose wrong, he'd definitely end up screwed. But if he made decent choices, there was a chance he might make it out all right.

Like Steve did.

We both could.

"Vega," I said, "I guarantee I'll be here to protect your neck and help you make the right moves."

"We should ask Steve," Vega said.

"Ask him what?"

"You know, about what he did to survive, get where he is. Maybe he has a blueprint—like the ones inside your

Lego kits—but his blueprint is on how to survive St. Nick projects."

I laughed.

But we agreed to talk to Steve. Especially if he had any ideas about dealing with Harp and Gully.

I scoped across the water and remembered again that we lived on an actual island. But there was something else too. Kids like us, me and Vega and Rose, were our own islands, living in a mad river.

We had to look out for ourselves.

"Thanks, man," Vega told me. "You manned up."

And then Vega just started sobbing his eyes out. Real hard, long sobs like I had done in the Bronx at that club. Like you cry when you're a rug rat. The kind of crying that makes you breathe all messed up and you feel like you're about to die of suffocation.

He almost did die, carrying that gun.

All I could do was stand there beside him, with my hand on his shoulder, until he slowed down and started breathing regular.

Breathing was about the only thing regular about how we lived.

36

"What you mean, she left?" I said.

Ali swiveled away in his office chair to face his desktop computer. He jiggled the mouse beside his keyboard to get rid of the screen saver. He pivoted back toward me.

"Like I said, Rosamund Major is gone," Mr. Ali repeated.

"But," I started, "she was here last week."

Ali nodded. "Child services got her over the weekend." He stood up to shut the door to his office. "Look here, Lolly, I'm not supposed to be telling you all of Big Rose's business—"

"*Rose,*" I corrected. "She don't like to be called *Big* Rose."

Ali nodded again. He sat down. His crooked face was tense. "I'm only telling you this because I know that you and Rosamund developed something special—"

"She's my friend," I said.

"Yeah, I know. Okay, man. Rose is different from the rest of you. She wasn't even supposed to be here, but we took her into this after-school because she'd been kicked out of several other programs. Got into clashes with other kids."

"They tease her," I said.

He nodded. "We took her here because her grandmother said she had no other alternatives. Betty had been homeschooling her for years. Got special permission from the city. But Betty was also able to prevent them from officially testing whether her granddaughter was a special-needs child. So Rose didn't really get the kind of attention that was necessary. She fell through the cracks."

"Rose ain't autistic."

Ali shook his head. "Turns out that after testing her, child services said she does fall on the spectrum for autism. For years, her grandmother had been denying it, telling Rose she was just like everybody else, but a couple weeks ago we were finally able to get Rose tested. Child services relocated her to Mount Vernon, just north of the city. There's a good school up there, near some relatives."

"Mr. Ali, *you* got Rose taken from her gran?"

Now he was talking to his computer screen, though it was meant for me: "Rose had to go, Lolly. Her grandmother wasn't up to raising her here. As much as Betty wanted to, she just couldn't handle it. How they lived wasn't good. Rose needed help. She's got some cousins up in Mount Vernon. They can take better care of her, at least until her grandmother gets things sorted out."

He stared at me.

"Rose is different," I said.

"Yeah," said Ali. "In fact, they say she can probably go to college someday."

"I think she *should* go to college," I said. "Become an engineer."

"Well, we'll see," he said.

The weird thing, he told me, was that Rose's gran keeping her out of the system for so long had actually helped Rose learn to relate to other people. Kids with Rose's type of autism, he said, sometimes have trouble communicating. They can be cut off from the world because they don't know how to talk to it.

Ali said, "Without Betty homeschooling her, putting her in after-school programs with regular kids, Rose might not've been as developed socially as she is today. She learned how to talk to others, how to read their body language. . . ."

"She doesn't like it when you point."

Ali nodded. "That's a trigger for her. But she's learning. Being out of the system forced her to refine those social skills on her own."

"And now you just plugged her into that system, Mr. Ali."

"It's better, Lolly," he said. "Because of *my* condition, when I was her age my parents tried to hide me away. I didn't get the medical help I needed until I was grown and the damage was difficult to reverse."

Was that why Ali had been mad at his father? I wondered.

"It's not too late for Rose," Ali said. "She's young. And you helped her a lot, you know. You helped her find a way to express herself, to touch the world around her in a different sort of way. Trust me, Lolly. It's her time."

I wasn't sure.

It was a nice-looking, clean building on a nice, clean block.

Lots of trees on this block.

In fact, the trees lining both sides of the street bent over toward one another so that when you glanced down the way, it looked like you were staring into a green cave made of tree branches.

The small sign above the buzzer said PLEASE RING BELL AND PRESS 9 AND #.

I did that.

Pretty soon somebody opened the front door and cracked the screen. It was a tall, dark-skinned Black dude. He stared down at me. He looked like I had just woke him up.

"Rosamund Major? She ain't here," he said after I had told him why I was there. "They went to the movies."

"Not here?" I asked him. I looked behind him and saw a small living room, with classroom desks farther back in another room. "She was supposed to be here. I spoke to Rodney this morning. He said she would be here."

"That was *you*?" he said. "I'm Rodney. I'm sorry, man. I forgot her class had a day trip this afternoon."

"I came all the way from Harlem."

"Harlem to Mount Vernon, huh?" He scrunched his face and yawned. "Sorry about that, man. Rosamund ain't here, though."

I probably sat on the front steps of that building for an hour waiting on Rose. She never showed.

This place in Mount Vernon was where Rose was now spending her afternoons in classes and learning. It was called her day school.

In the evenings she was staying with cousins who lived nearby.

It seemed nice up here.

Sitting on the steps there, I watched a green leaf drop down from one of the tree branches above me. I wondered if she was happy here.

Daddy honked the horn of his blue van, parked across the street. I sighed, grabbed the little gift I had brought for Rose and stood.

He had a clown gig today, I knew, and had to drive us back into New York or he'd be late.

· ✦ ✚ ✦ ·

He took his time driving down Rose's block, even though I knew he was in a hurry to get back to the city. As Daddy's van crept along the quiet street, we both crooked our necks up to stare at the ceiling of the tree cave.

His girlfriend, Heike, was stretched out across the backseat of the van, eyes shut. If you looked close at her eyelids you could see little blue veins on them, which I thought was weird.

"I'm sorry about your friend, Wallace," Daddy said, still staring up at all the green.

I shrugged.

"It's tough when a trueheart moves away," he said. "I recollect years ago, when I was younger than your age now, living in Trinidad, and my good friend Tommy and his family left the island to come here to the U.S. Little Thomas Crawley! *Ah,* I cried and cried like a baby. I never will forget that."

I thought about my father crying like a baby. "Did you ever see him again?"

Daddy shook his head. "I was a child! How was I supposed to travel thousands of miles from Trinidad to here to visit my buddy?" He laughed.

In the backseat, Heike groaned and turned over on her side.

"Mount Vernon's only fifteen miles from Harlem," I said. "But with no subways running here, it might as well be Trinidad, Daddy."

He grunted. "What you think *this* is? Sir Wallace, my van is your van! We will come back so you can meet your friend. *Word is born.*"

Daddy Rachpaul grabbed my head and shook it. I smiled and thought about what Mr. Ali had said about starting over fresh with my father.

Right then, it seemed like it could happen. I felt like Prince Stellar of the Star Drivers, reunited with his alien dad after years and years. Maybe my space stories weren't just a bunch of stories after all.

Maybe I could predict the future.

Or help create it.

Our van stalled at a stop sign on the next block. A line of about eight young people marched in front of us on the crosswalk.

At first they caught my attention because one of them was wearing a long red cape with a yellow bandanna covering his head, with eyeholes cut into it so he could see. He looked like a superhero, walking in these long, awkward strides. Dude must'a been twenty years old, dressed like that, and it wasn't nowhere near Halloween.

I got tense and started to scan the crowd.

All of them crossing in front of us was unusual. Some of

them had older people walking beside them, guiding them along. Others paced by themselves.

And then I saw Rose's big head at the end of the line.

That was her, stomping along the crosswalk in front of our van, looking like she was skipping rope on the moon. Her upper lip tucked into her bottom one.

"Rose!" I yelled, and jumped out of the van.

I ran up to her on the other side of the street. I stopped just before I reached her and just stood there, staring at her. She looked back at me and blinked. Then looked down the block both ways, like she was trying to figure out where she was.

"Rose!" I said again. "We drove up here! I thought I missed you!"

One of the older people walked up toward us. The rest of the group had paused on the sidewalk.

"Rosamund, do you know this boy?" the older person asked.

Rose didn't say nothing. She stared at the ground, but kept glancing up at me.

"Yes," she said, and grinned. "That's Lolly. We build cities."

"Oh, yes!" the older person said. "You talk about him."

I only had a couple of minutes to chat with Rose before they said she had to go. We were holding up the whole group. And some of them were starting to get anxious. My father honking the horn didn't help that situation either.

Before climbing back in the van, I gave Rose a quick hug and handed her the gift I brought for her. It was a little book of poems by this poet named Safia Elhillo. Sunny's moms had helped me pick it out because the poet was positive for Black women.

She was a new poet. I hoped Rose would like her.

Rose squeezed my present in front of her chest and watched us drive off.

I was glad to see her again.

All those talks I had had with Mr. Ali had been good. They had helped me, I guess.

But what me and Rose had gone through together over the past few months had been the main cure for me. She had helped heal me the most.

That and wanting to do right for my mother.

Seeing Rose there in our van's rearview mirror, standing underneath those green tree limbs, didn't seem right to me, though. Sure, it was pretty up here on her block, but it wasn't Harlem; it wasn't St. Nick Houses.

It wasn't home.

37

Lying flat on my back on the beady quilt in my bedroom, I was listening through the walls. Ma and Yvonne had been out there in the living room screaming at each other for a bit.

When Yvonne had first come over, thirty minutes ago, they had started going at it so loud that I knew the whole building must'a overheard. That dude Concrete down in the courtyard seven stories below had probably understood them.

Now they had calmed down a little. No more shouting, just stressed voices. After it had got completely quiet on the other side of the wall, I got scared thinking they might'a strangled each other.

Until I heard a knock on my door. It was Yvonne. She strolled into my room with a funny expression on her face. She looked kind of guilty.

Yvonne glanced to the opposite corner of my bedroom, where Jermaine's old bed used to sit. We had got rid of it the other day. It had been tough, but I finally told Ma that I needed it out.

I felt better after we had moved it to storage.

My room felt lighter.

Red-faced, Yvonne plopped down on the edge of my bed.

I laid there with my hands folded behind my head, listening to her talk and explain herself and tell me why she had done what she had done. I had kind of known, but it was helpful to hear it direct from her own mouth.

"I'm sorry, Loll," Yvonne said. "I did the wrong thing. Almost got you in trouble too. They were never trashing those Legos. I took them because of how you were back then. Right after your brother had passed. I shouldn't'a done it. But you were so dejected, I thought they would make you feel better."

"They did. They did make me feel a *whole* lot better."

She nodded. "Even after your depression had started to lift, I just couldn't stop bringing you more Legos. Back then, seeing you happier—and your ma worry less about you—gave me joy." She scratched her yellow Mohawk. "So . . . I guess, after a while, I was sneaking them to make me feel good too. Like I was really doing something. I couldn't stop giving you more."

"I understand, Yvonne. I ain't mad at you. It's one of the coolest things anybody ever did for me."

Yvonne laughed.

"And I need to thank you," I said, sitting up. "Not for you stealing. But just before I found out what you had done, I was about to make a decision. And I think it would'a been a bad one. One that might'a changed me for good. But you getting caught, and all the upset and drama it caused, helped me to deep-think. Made me see things clear like they were."

"So you forgive me?" she asked.

I shrugged. "I ain't got nothing to forgive."

She smiled. We bumped fists and that was that.

After Yvonne had left me alone in my room, I sat on the floor admiring some of the pieces of Harmonee that I had saved. The leftovers.

Next time, I thought, *I'm gonna do it bigger.*

I started to reach for my sketchbook, but instead slid out the tablet Daddy Rachpaul had bought me for Late Christmas. There was an interesting graphics app I had downloaded and installed. This program let you draw and design things in your tablet like you were really building stuff in the real world.

Sitting there on my rug in my bedroom, I started designing blueprints for a brand-new city, with brand-new buildings and totally new stories.

What would I call it?

I got into it, feeling pretty much like I had felt that night when I had decided to break apart all of my old Lego kits and start telling the House of Moneekrom story.

Excited.

Hopeful.

I had ideas.

Man, did I have ideas.

· ✦ ✦ ✦ ·

It was one of those crazy warm May spring days that reminds you that summer is coming and about everything that comes along with summer. 125th Street was full of folks, crowded all together, moving, shaking, shouting and rushing everywhere.

Vega and me was walking the sidewalk toward Applebee's. Ma and Yvonne was strolling real sluggish behind us. They were both moving too slow, their cargo shorts and T-shirts sticking to them.

My mother had agreed to treat all of us to dinner this time, even Vega, which had made both Yvonne and Vega very joyful.

And Vega was back to his old self again after our experience beside the Harlem River. I guess, sometimes, all it really takes is a real proper cry to solve all of your problems. Or at least make you forget all of the problems you still got.

He hadn't mentioned Harp and Gully lately, but I knew, sooner or later, just like that miserable winter weather, them boys would return.

I did still have Rockit's phone number. He had said to call him if I ever needed help. But I decided against that, thinking that if anybody needed help, it would be Rockit. He was doing the same old stuff as everybody else like him; he would wind up in the same spot.

We'd both asked to talk to Steve about how to deal with Harp and Gully. He would know what to do. Out of everybody we knew growing up in the projects, Steve had survived it. For himself, he had made a bad situation better.

"Ms. Sue!" Vega yelled, even though Ma was right beside him.

"Vega, Vega," Ma said. "Cool the noise, baby. Don't speak in decibels."

"Lolly said I missed you in your dress," he told her. "How come I never see you in one?"

Ma thought on this a minute, then said, "I ain't that type of mom."

All of a sudden I spun around and started walking backward, so I could laser Ma and Yvonne in their eyeballs.

"Ma!" I yelled.

"We right *here*, sugar," she said, like she was growing annoyed. "You ain't got to yell."

"Everybody goes to Applebee's," I said. "Let's do something different."

Vega spun around and started walking backward too.

We both laughed at each other. I thought about my St. Nick partners, him and Sunny—all they did was argue! I really hoped that mess would stop. They were both my friends and I wanted to laugh with both of them.

Sunny wasn't so bad.

She had tried to save our coyote, which was something cool.

Earlier, I had made the mistake of telling Vega about that thing Sunny had done right before she had jumped on the elevator. How she had made my skin get hot in the hallway.

When he had heard this, Vega just laughed and laughed and laughed and laughed and laughed. I was embarrassed, but it was good to hear him laugh again.

Then he started rolling around on my bed, like he was about to throw up.

"I'm regurgitating! I'm regurgitating!" he kept yelling.

Playing around. He always played too much. Something had told me he wouldn't understand. Finally, he asked me if I had liked her doing what she did.

I remember shrugging at him. "I don't know," I told him.

"Something different?" Yvonne finally asked me, back on 125th Street. "What you got in mind, Loll?"

"Walking backwards, you gonna fool around and fall flat on your backside," Ma warned us.

I said, "Let's take the four train downtown. I know a really flavory food truck that sells arepas. We can sit in Union Square and eat 'em."

"Downtown? Arepas?" Yvonne asked. She was suspicious. I could tell.

"Arepas are like little hot sandwiches," Vega said. "Tasty."

"They're cheap and good too," I added. Ma thought on this for a minute, then cracked an immense grin.

"Okay, Lolly," she said. "Let's try something different. And *you* need to open up to new experiences, *Yvonne.*" Ma elbowed her. Yvonne sucked her teeth.

"And I don't wanna be called Lolly no more," I told my mother. "My name is Wallace Rachpaul."

"Oh, is it really?" Ma said, acting like I had just asked to be called Prince Stellar.

"I wanna go by my real name from now on," I said, and spun back around, walking forward.

I thought about Rosamund and wondered what new thing she was building now. I had decided to forgive Mr. Ali for turning her in to Child Services. I believed he thought he was doing the right thing, even if his right thing might be the wrong thing.

A week after I had visited Rose at her day school, I got an email from her. It was short and to the point: she really didn't like Mount Vernon and missed Gran, though her grandma visited her a lot.

Rose also said she didn't like the poetry book I had gave her.

I didn't need her telling me that.

But the coolest thing about Rose's email was the attachment. She included that photo of me and her standing on the cobblestones in front of the diamond house in the Meatpacking District. She wasn't smiling in the picture either. She wasn't that type of girl.

Out of all those pictures of buildings I had took, this was the only one that had survived. My parents still hadn't bought me a new phone.

I had lost a lot and learned a lot since this time last year. And despite my skinny muscles, I had discovered my own superpower. Building thingamajigs fresh out my head.

You gotta learn to do something new. I wished Jermaine could'a been around now to know that. Walking down 125th Street, I missed him more than anything. I wished he was here with us.

I wasn't mad at him no more, for trying to get me to join his crew. I'd been deep-thinking a lot about why he actually tried that. After having told me years before to stay away.

It had to do with who he had started to roll with, I thought. The folks you hang out with can raise you up or bring you down low. Over time, they can make you think a certain way—change who you really are.

Jermaine didn't realize that, I guess.

Or didn't remember it when he needed to.

Like Mr. Ali had suggested, I had decided to remember everything good about my brother—keep him close to my heart.

I had decided that whenever I felt like I needed to chat with him, tell him what was on my mind, I would go to that overlook at the upper tip of Harlem where Vega and me had tossed the gun. That little spot on the Harlem River that faced the Bronx.

The Boogie Down.

It had all ended there for Jermaine.

And from that overlook, I would talk to my brother. That place would be my exclusive hideaway just to remember him.

I smiled, reminiscing about him now.

And I also remembered a cold, mean time when I was stepping down this same street, and it had been impossible for me to smile about anything. . . .

That was *loooong* past now.

Since then I had learned the most important thing: the decisions you make can become your life. Your choices are you.

AUTHOR'S NOTE

I love language.

In the city where I live, New York, there are millions of people who speak many different languages. Sometimes, as I walk about my city or take the subway or ride the bus, I listen carefully. I listen to what people say and how they say it.

If you want to be a storyteller, it's important to understand other people's points of view. We often feel that we *must* say what we must say. It's also crucial, however, to listen to other voices. Listening, I think, is the best way to learn about those who differ from you.

Reading is a form of listening.

One of the reasons that I wanted to write *The Stars Beneath Our Feet* is that there aren't enough books that speak with the voices of the characters in my story. Though I grew up in suburban Missouri—very different from the Harlem of my central character, Lolly Rachpaul—as an adult, I lived in Harlem for many years and heard voices like his firsthand.

African American Vernacular, or Black English, is as varied as the people who speak it. Indeed, a slang word in one Harlem neighborhood may not even be used in another Harlem neighborhood just a few blocks away. I am certain that many of the young Harlem readers of my book will point this fact out to me, or mention that some of the slang words I use are outdated.

In today's social media culture, words that are popular now can sometimes become unpopular by next week. My sincere hope is that *The Stars Beneath Our Feet* will be read and enjoyed for many years to come. In writing it, I tried to use words from African American Vernacular that would paint a timeless picture of one aspect of our Black culture.

But I hope that what I've created will have significance universally.

The journey of self-discovery that Lolly follows throughout *The Stars Beneath Our Feet* is one that many of us undertake. When I lost my brother Brian in 2011, I was struck with grief. Similarly, Lolly is challenged with accepting his own brother's passing. The emotions that Lolly goes through in my story are, in some ways, a reflection of what I went through.

Loss is something all of us must experience and weather. There's a little bit of Lolly inside of me, inside of you. There's a little bit of Lolly inside of all of us.

Thank you for listening to his story.

David Barclay Moore

Brooklyn, 2017

ACKNOWLEDGMENTS

Thanks to God and to my late parents, John N. Sr. & Leanora Moore. Thank you for being the most loving role models, for sacrificing so much and for making me who I am today. Thanks also to my sister and her family, Leanora Moore-Beulah and Mark, Nicole & Ryan Beulah; and to my brother and his family, John N. Jr., Deandra, Braxton, Brandon & Brooke Moore. Thanks to my late grandmother, Leanora Bolton, for the gift of loving books. Additional thanks to all of my other relatives.

Thanks to everyone else who's shown me love and support over the years—including Asari Beale; "Bealesy" & Octavia; Lloyd Boston; Brooklyn Public Library; Bruce & Tenzin; Suzette Burgess; Geoffrey Canada; Hassan Daniel; Matt de la Peña; Raymel Garcia; Timothy Greenfield-Sanders (photographer extraordinaire! thanks for making me look better than I really do); Stephen Sean Hewett; Jennifer Hunt; Betina Jean-Louis; R. Kikuo Johnson; John

R. Keene (simply the best); Steven A. King; Mariann Lai, MS Ed, SAS, BCBA, LBA, executive director of Autism Early Enrichment Services, NYC; Hannah Mann; Maria T. Middleton; Tracie Morris; the sorely missed Walter Dean Myers (thanks for creating spaces for so many of us and for the lunches and tête-à-têtes you treated me to); New York Public Library; Ndlela Nkobi (always there!); Rosomond Osborne; Milly Perez; Carlos Sirah (can't stop, won't stop); Patricia Stewart; The Three Latinas (Connie Polanco, Iris "Mookie" Torres and Erika Rivera); Etefia Umana Sr. (Experience Unlimited! Love you!) and his family—Etefia Jr., Sissy and Zora Umana, mother Joetta Umana & the rest of the Umana clan; Barry White of Barry White Men's Grooming, NYC; Jaime Wolf (*"Mon dieu!"*) of Pelosi Wolf Effron & Spates, NYC; Jacqueline Woodson; Yaddo; and the beautiful people of Harlem.

A special thanks to my simpatico super-editor, Nancy Siscoe, and everyone else at Knopf who supported and worked on this book. You showed so much faith in me.

Aside from me, the person most responsible for bringing *The Stars Beneath Our Feet* into the world is my agent, Steven Malk of Writers House, who is "literally" a throwback to a bygone era of publishing (in a good way). Steve, your intelligence, guidance, savvy and belief in me from the very beginning were and are invaluable.

And an enduring thank-you for my beloved brother Brian Patrick Moore, who is with me in spirit and to whom this book is dedicated.

"Ciao for now!" as Brian would have said.

ABOUT THE AUTHOR

David Barclay Moore was born and raised in Missouri. After studying creative writing at Iowa State University, film at Howard University in Washington, D.C., and language studies at l'Université de Montpellier in France, David moved to New York City, where he has served as communications coordinator for Geoffrey Canada's Harlem Children's Zone and communications manager for Quality Services for the Autism Community.

He has received grants from the Ford Foundation, the Jerome Foundation, Yaddo, and the Wellspring Foundation. He was also a semifinalist for the Sundance Screenwriters Lab.

David now lives, works, and explores in Brooklyn, N.Y. You can read more about him at DavidBarclayMoore.com or follow him on Twitter and Instagram at @dbarclaymoore.